Christmas In Pilaf

Food For The Soul

André Bernier

Dedicated to anyone and everyone who
dares too believe,
dares to discover,
dares to love,
and therefore dares to live life well.

Foreword

I always enjoy a writing challenge. It's even better if that challenge dovetails with a cliff-hanger that leaves your audience wanting more. I must admit, I had a great deal of fun creating an interesting twist to the conclusion in Book 2. The last two sentences were questions, ones that remained completely unanswered for quite some time. Let me explain.

Readers were vocal, tongue-in-cheek, and cried foul. I even saw someone shaking a fist, telling me that I had better answer those two questions somewhere in Book 3. I just grinned and told him I would do my best.

Some of my best writing, in my humble opinion, is when I intentionally paint myself into a literary corner. Why? It forces me to come up with creative ideas to find a way out. There have been so many readers who figured I knew exactly how I was going to resolve the ending in Book 2. Nothing could be farther from the truth. For months, I tried getting myself out of the literary corner but couldn't find a pathway that would serve as a satisfying stepping stone to the next set of adventures in the cozy little town of Pilaf, Ohio. In April 2016, I accepted a wonderful opportunity to help our first church home in Ohio, serving as interim pastor. Between my weekday duties as an on-air meteorologist and weekend commitment leading Chesterland Baptist Church, writing a follow-up book for 2016 was simply out of the question. I actually breathed a sigh of relief. This bought me the time I needed to figure out how I was going to navigate my way out of that tight literary corner.

Every month or so, a new idea came to me. But the proverbial light bulb did nothing more than illuminate one dead end after another. Thinking inside the box was not working well, so I went hunting outside the box. That's when things started to click. I was finally able to craft an exciting bridge that would escort you from the uncertainty of those last two questions of Pilaf, Book 2 to what promises to be a delightful, and always eventful, Christmas season in the little Ohio town that you've grown to love.

Prologue

The contrast was stark. A half-eaten, store-bought brownie, still in its torn wrapper, was surrounded by several high-end foodie magazines showcasing such delicacies as Chateaubriand, Beef Wellington, and Lobster Thermidor. On the other side of the heavy, vintage work desk, the contrast continued with a well-organized stack of photographs that balanced the space, with very little beyond a business card holder in the middle.

John Rowe's hand, palm open and relaxed, was resting on his desk only inches from the plastic-looking brownie. He was snoring when there was a light knock at his door. His eyes opened. He stared straight ahead not seeming to focus on anything, as if he was in a trance. Only when there was a second knock at his door did his head finally turn. His inadvertent nap was so deep, that he awoke confused, briefly forgetting where he was.

"Who's there?"

John's wife, Eloise, gently peeked inside the home office door, "Who else would it be?"

She entered quietly as she had done this dozens, if not hundreds of times before. Noticing the scene into which she walked, Eloise simply pointed to the half-eaten brownie from some unidentified rest area vending machine. She came to a stop near the corner of John's desk and stood motionless.

"I know, I know," he resigned, "processed sugar and carbs make me crash faster than you can read a recipe. Had you not caught me closing my eyes for just a moment, you would have never known."

"Closing your eyes for a moment? Even Spela, who is at the opposite end of the hallway, heard your classic snore," Eloise said, making reference to their twenty-year-old, forever snoozing feline. "I'm amazed that such a sound never wakes you!"

"I wasn't snoring," John insisted.

Eloise could not contain the humor she found in her husband's reply. Her laughter was mixed with snorting that would startle even the most seasoned stand-up comic.

"Not funny, Eloise. So aside from my fictional snoring, is there anything else that brought you around to check up on me?"

Eloise finally admitted that John's snoring was not the reason for her visit. It was twofold. The first was to ask if he had sampled the homemade apple pie that he brought home from his road trip. She could not resist and had the first slice. Immediately, John was wide awake. Expecting that reaction, Eloise smiled. Knowing how to get the full attention of a former real estate agent turned popular media culinary critic is "as easy as pie". The fact that Eloise did not allow her husband to sample the first slice did not bother him at all. He was much more curious about her appraisal.

"And...?," he asked.

"It's amazing. There's something in there that I can't put my finger on. Perhaps your taste buds can reveal that mystery."

It was a challenge he would accept after dinner, something that Eloise said would be ready in thirty minutes. That gave John enough time to call Adrienne, a realtor with whom he made an offer on a grand Victorian house far away from city life. After almost a decade of going with the fast flow of the busy metropolis, both John and Eloise agreed it was time to find a home that overlooked a yard and trees, something they missed from his days as a realtor. John had so well established his television culinary program, that he could now produce the show from any location, and head into the city only for short intervals to film the program. Eventually, his endgame would be to film in a more scenic location within driving distance of their dream home in the country.

Eloise retreated to the kitchen to put the finishing touches on her own version of Pâté Chinois, an elegant version of Shepherd's Pie, something the English established as a down-home staple as early as the 1790s when potatoes were introduced as an edible crop.

Her husband's notoriety as a culinary expert never affected her creative juices in their kitchen. While it was John who had the high-profile connection to food, Eloise's kitchen savvy was equally magnificent. They met on the kitchen set of a local variety program in Ohio called New Day Cleveland when John was beginning to gain fame for his unique recipes. Eloise was one of the producers. She was watching the segment from the control room and decided almost immediately that she would introduce herself after the segment was over. During that encounter, John offered her some of his coconut-lime shrimp to try. That sample was the start of a perfect match.

It was John's custom to stay out of the kitchen when Eloise was whipping up a meal for the two of them. It had nothing to do with food preparation at all, but rather her choice of music. Much to John's annoyance, Eloise would almost invariably tune the kitchen speakers to a contemporary country radio station in Nashville. John preferred classical or smooth jazz. Country music of any kind, contemporary or not, distracted him. It wasn't so much the musical style as it was the lyrical content. He simply could not get past some of the hillbilly jargon. It's something Eloise was able to ignore, choosing to focus on the often upbeat country arrangements as she tapped and twirled around the kitchen, adding a little of this or that to the bubbling pots and pans on the stove.

When dinner was ready, Eloise called Spela. He obediently stolled into the kitchen and looked up for further instructions.

"Go get John. It's time for dinner."

As if he understood perfectly, Spela wandered out of the kitchen and down the hall to John's office. No more than a minute later, John appeared with Spela in his arms. He had done his job well. By then Eloise had already made a music selection change that filled the kitchen and nearby dining room with smooth jazz. John's gentle smile was confirmation that he was already enjoying the ambience.

They moved to the dinner table. John clasped his hands and Eloise closed her eyes and looked down as John said grace. This was not just a home ritual. Whether they were enjoying a quiet meal at home or out with clients, television producers, or advertisers at a loud, busy restaurant, John did not even consider taking a nibble of the most tantalizing appetizer without thanking God for their food. Of course, there were times when the prayer was said in desperation, mainly when they were served something they could not identify. That's when the prayer went from "thank you" mode to "please help me get through this" mode. Tonight's prayer was sweet, gentle, and thankful.

As they began to enjoy the Pâté Chinois, John's body language gave away his eagerness to share something with Eloise. Naturally, she wondered why John was acting this way, but just like the elusive ingredient in the apple pie, she could not put her finger on it. After several forkfuls and several long sips of Chardonnay, John finally paused and took a breath. His smile revealed that whatever he was about to make known, Eloise could relax. It was something good.

"I just got off the phone with Adrienne before Spela came in to get me."

"Oh?"

John reached for what appeared to be a face-down photo. When he turned it over, he winked and smiled.

"Our offer was accepted," he beamed as he handed Eloise the photo of the Victorian house in the country. After that revelation, their mealtime conversation did not drift from the joy of knowing that they would soon be living their dream. They were both anxious to live in a place where they could once again sit on a porch on mild evenings to watch life go by.

Eloise had a new spring in her step when she insisted on clearing the table without help. John pulled the big, country apple pie closer so he could prepare two slices. Wasting little time, John was anxious to sample the treasure he brought home from the endearing town that would soon be their home.

Eloise was right about the pie. There was a taste that was eluding John's refined culinary detection. Whatever it was made John go back for another sliver. His second piece did not offer any more clues than the first bite. Despite that, one thing remained clear. It was outstanding!

John and Eloise retreated to the breakfast counter to split an evening cup of coffee from a small

French press. John had carefully placed all of the photos of their newly purchased Victorian house on the counter. They lingered over each one with such focus that they missed Spela's bold move from one of the dining room chairs, to the dining table. He was headed for the apple pie.

John and Eloise heard an unusual sound, like a small piece of metal jingling. They both turned to see Spela on the dining room table, inches away from the apple pie, playing with something shiny. From the small claw marks on the pie, it appeared that the shiny something came from the center of the apple pie. What was it? Spela would not let them see it. He picked it up with his teeth and hopped off the table and scampered out of the room. There were few places he could go, so it was not long before Eloise spotted the object of Spela's delight. She picked it up from the corner of their walk-in closet where it was too dark to see. It felt like a ring of some sort. As Eloise brought it back to the kitchen, the overhead light confirmed her initial thought. Not only was it a ring, it was a stunning engagement ring with a large, sparkling diamond.

When Eloise showed it to John, his jaw dropped. The topic of conversation was no longer the pie, but what apparently was buried in the middle of it.

"Who in the world would bake an apple pie with an expensive engagement ring hidden in the middle? Where did you say you bought this apple pie?"

John replied, "In the little country town where we just bought our Victorian home, a place called Pilaf. There was this apple pie baking contest on New Year's Eve, and I won the silent auction for this one. By then it was getting pretty late. At the risk of not making my late-night flight back to New York, I took my pie from the emcee and raced to the car," he explained "I'm glad I did because another few minutes lingering at the church hall and I would have missed my flight home. Cleveland is nice, but I didn't want to spend New Year's Day in an unfamiliar city without you."

Eloise was sidetracked for a moment.

"Pilaf? There's a town called Pilaf in Ohio? Why Pilaf?"

John chuckled as he tried giving his wife the CliffsNotes version of a rather complex storyline. In his years as a Vermont realtor, he always had a friendly competition going with another realtor in the office, Adrienne Camp. The top seller of the month would usually be one of the two. Aside from their success in the real estate business, each had something else bubbling under the radar. For John, it was his love for cooking and showing people how to cook. For Adrienne, it was her longing to return to her home state of Ohio. When John announced that he was leaving the realty business to take a chance on hosting his own culinary program on a local New York City station, Adrienne, too, announced that she was leaving to pursue her own dream of moving back to Ohio.

Nearly a decade later, Adrienne was doing well as a realtor in Pilaf. She loved the slow and steady pace of life in her home state, not far from New Bedford, Ohio, her childhood hometown. She had recently become the selling agent for a beautiful Victorian home a short walking distance from Bailey's Country Store. After meeting with the owners and touring the home, Adrienne realized just how strikingly similar it was to John and Eloise's Victorian home in Burke Ridge, Vermont. So similar, that she simply had to locate John to show him photos. As soon as the photos had audience with John, given his sense of increasing fatigue, he was instantly enamored with the thought of taking control of his own daily routine. It was time.

Eloise was fascinated but not surprised with John's tale. It was no secret that he was considering a dramatic change when his network contract came up for renewal. He even talked about hanging up his television apron if network executives would not go along with a slower, more deliberate filming itinerary. Now, with all of their personal pieces in place, it was the network's turn. John hoped they would embrace his new plan, but was ready to make this move with or without them.

With the dazzling ring still between Eloise's fingers, her focus returned to the oddity of having an apple pie deliver an obviously expensive engagement ring. After tossing out several wild guesses, John remembered the small envelope that each pie had for the successful bidder. Perhaps it held an important clue that would lead them to some answers. The only problem was that he could not remember what happened to the envelope. He was almost certain he brought it home, but everything else was a blur, similar to the somewhat jumbled desk in his home office. As much as he hated the thought of weeding out his office, it was the next logical step in trying to locate the notecard. Thankfully, the French press coffee was enough to prevent both of them from setting aside that task until another day, a day that has a habit of never arriving.

Ordinarily, trading chaos for order in John's office was not a pleasant task. Tonight was different. As they began sifting through the messy stacks in John's office, the daydream of moving into their new Victorian home gave the task an element of joy. Fifteen minutes had passed when Spela came in. He stayed by the door where John's coat was hanging. He watched for a few minutes as if perplexed by this unusual evening activity, then stretched upward on his hind legs and began pawing at John's coat. John saw him do this but paid little attention to him. Spela repeated this same odd stretch several times, each time walking over as he wondered if they saw what he was doing. Eventually, he became bored and slowly walked out of John's office.

Several hours had passed. The office looked amazing, but they were not able to locate the notecard that John insisted came with the pie. Spela had been absent for a couple of hours when he reappeared at the door, standing by John's coat. Spela stretched on the coat once more. This time, Spela caught something with his paw, quickly flicking at it as if he had cornered a mouse. Eloise saw something sticking out of the coat pocket and walked over. Spela returned to his princely posture near the coat as if he had finally accomplished his goal of helping.

Eloise looked closely at the pocket's opening and saw the corner of an envelope. When she pulled out the notecard-sized envelope, she looked up at John and waived it.

"Is this what we've been trying to locate for the past few hours?"

"Of course," John exclaimed, "that's where I put it when I first walked out of the church hall with the pie!"

Eloise handed it to John. His letter opener was now very easy to find given their evening cleaning frenzy. Once opened, John read the notecard:

To my one and only Marcie –

My apple pie is nowhere near as phenomenal as yours. It will never win this fun contest. But I'm hoping that this one-of-a-kind pie will win your heart. What you find in the center is a token of my commitment to love you forever. Will you be my forever bride?

Love, Arborio

John and Eloise looked at one another, without saying a word. The grave realization that they were part of something that went very, very wrong stunned them into silence until John finally spoke.

"Uh, oh."

"What do we do now?" Eloise queried.

John picked up the phone and called Adrienne. It was late, but this was an emergency. Fortunately, Adrienne was still awake, something unusual in a town that turns in not long after the sun goes down. John explained his sequence of events. Even though he knew that Adrienne was not at the pie baking contest that night, he asked if she was aware of any proposals that went awry. Indeed she was. Who in Pilaf didn't know? Since the rest of the town was asleep, Adrienne would wait until morning to pay a visit to Pilaf Elementary to inform the newly engaged couple that Miss Miller's ring was not only in New York City, but in the safe hands of one of the country's most famous television chefs.

One of Adrienne's first stops the following morning was Bailey's Country Store, Pilaf's news hub. Once she told Danny about the unusual phone call from America's chef, John Rowe, the happy news quickly spread. Adrienne knew that she would have enough time to walk over to Pilaf Elementary to give Pilaf's celebrated couple the news first hand. In the weeks that followed, the townspeople were giddy with excitement.

Several weeks later when John and Eloise arrived in town to close on their new Victorian home, Adrienne arranged for them to meet Mr. Rayburn and Miss Miller at Bailey's. She was able to keep it quiet enough to prevent Bailey's from being occupied by the entire town. Eloise put the ring into Mr. Rayburn's hand so he could finally slide the beautiful ring onto Miss Miller's finger. At that moment they realized they were sitting in the same seats where they shared a slice of pie during their first lunch break together, the very spot where Cupid's arrow hit a bullseye.

Food For The Soul

"You can't escape the food you had as a child. In times of stress, what do you dream about? Your mother's clam chowder. It's security, comfort. It brings you home."

Jacques Pépin

Sunday, November 19, 2017, 7:22 AM

That amazing apple candle from the big apple pie baking contest is all I could think about this morning. I warmed the ambience of the kitchen by lighting an apple pie scented candle on the kitchen counter while I reminisced. I'm not sure if there is something in the water that draws so many small miracles to Pilaf, or whether it's because we tend to pay greater attention to the wonder of God moving in our lives. Whatever it is, it makes me smile in ways I could have never imagined before buying Bailey's Country Store.

Lighting a candle or two, for no other reason but atmosphere on a quiet Sunday morning, brings a peaceful smile to my face. I'm sure the added contrast of staring out the window at the season's first snowfall adds to that cozy sensation. All that remains is some furball lap time from Sammy, while staring out at a wintry scene absent since April 15th. It's appropriate when you consider that Uncle

Ben forever tells everyone at Bailey's that he never puts away his winter implements until "tax day." Despite the two-inch snowfall that surprised even Stormy Windham, Uncle Ben was not the least bit nervous about declaring the winter season closed the next day. He sure was right. Less than a week later, Joel and Jessie wanted to wear shorts to school when temperatures zoomed past 80°F for nearly a week.

Sammy must be curled up sleeping in some warm nook, perhaps near one of the heating ducts. It's unusual that he has not yet made his presence known. It's just as well. My coffee mug is nearly empty and the snowy landscape insists on a second cup. If Sammy was sprawled out on my lap, a second cup would not be an option. There is an unwritten, but understood cat rule that when Sammy is on your lap, you are not to move. Any movement, no matter how slight, will result in a furball creatively distributing its weight in such a way that makes it nearly impossible to budge.

Sunday, November 19, 2017, 4:21 PM

I'm glad to see the Cleveland Browns doing better. Nonetheless, my interest has tempered over the years, not because of last season's near-winless record, but because I have purposefully restructured my Sunday afternoons removing television from the equation. That seems to be a trend, at least with football. Jennifer, a football fan, has a theory about this. Because the internet offers instant everything, we've grown impatient having to wait in between plays, official timeouts, injuries, and changes of possession. Interesting theory. She may be onto something.

The church was decorated for Christmas today. I liked it, but it wasn't unanimous within the congregation. The rebellion was actually cute. It came from little Annie Anderson. Even though she is almost 6 years old, she is no longer the little peanut who crawled into the church manger scene three years ago during Pastor O'Connor's message. Nevertheless, I don't think she will ever grow out of that title, even if she towers over all of us in time. Annie was quite vocal about the violation of playing Christmas music before Thanksgiving. Since Annie was born on Thanksgiving Day in 2011 (November 24), she enjoys being the center of attention until Thanksgiving has passed. Only then should

Christmas music be heard. She might have a hard time convincing George the mailman to wait until November 24th this year (which falls on a Friday). I've occasionally caught George "testing" his outdoor audio system as early as the first week of November, not that I snoop around George's place as the Christmas season approaches. Officer Caputo tries to convince people otherwise though.

Annie now has to share her birthday with two more people. Not a birthday, but an anniversary. Marcie and Arbie Rayburn will be celebrating their first anniversary on November 24th. Talk about unique. The circumstances that surrounded their engagement were so extraordinary, that they both decided that their wedding should be totally unconventional as well. I don't know of any other couple who tied the knot on Thanksgiving Day, let alone in the middle of a football stadium at halftime during an annual rival high school game! That's quite a play for the spotlight, but Annie didn't seem to mind sharing her birthday with two people she truly admired. After all, it was her strategy with an apple-shaped candle that proved the catalyst that now binds them together. This year, Annie's birthday and the Rayburn's anniversary will fall on a Friday. I heard some chatter at Bailey's about observing both in a fun way. No details yet.

Monday, November 20, 2017, 8:02 AM

Every time I think I miss the superfluous sounds of elementary school children becoming excited for the holiday season's approach, I have to stop myself. That is a sentiment which is filtered by time. Time is a powerful element that has the ability to sift some of the memorable holiday drama when Joel and Jessie were much younger. Very much like a fine wine in the process of developing into an impressive vintage, the early stages can lead any taster to believe that even time could not tame what was just sampled.

I can now chuckle at the thought of one of these moments that was far from amusing the year it happened. Joel was always our industrious engineer, even as a young tot. He developed quite a fascination with the strings of Christmas lights adorning the mantle and tree in the living room. He was always touching, moving, and tweaking their placement. One year, there was a lit string still on the floor, not having found its place on the tree. Jennifer called me to help her with something in the kitchen. After the task, we sat down at the breakfast counter for what seemed like only a moment. From the living room, giggling turned into laughter. It sounded delightfully benign until Jennifer and I walked through the living room door. Jennifer gasped. I was so shocked I couldn't utter a sound. Joel and Jessie's laughter continued as Joel exclaimed, "It's a halo!"

Joel used twisty-ties to attach the string of LED lights to Jessie's long, blonde hair on the crown of her head. It was actually stunning, worthy of many photos. Joel's engineering prowess and technique was so professional, that removing the twisty-ties one at a time took Jennifer and I over two hours. I had no idea why we had so many saved twisty-ties. To say that Jennifer and I were not amused would be putting it lightly. All this while Joel and Jessie giggled and squirmed to get away. That was a little more difficult for Jessie, who's halo was thankfully tethered. That's only one of many ghosts of Christmas past that come to mind. We've since kept the number of spare twisty-ties down to a handful. We both doubted we would see a repeat performance, but Jennifer and I were not about to take any chances.

Now that Joel and Jessie are growing and maturing, so is the way they express the joy of

Thanksgiving and Christmas. Their celebration is a bit more refined. No longer do we expect to see Jessie sporting an LED halo. The laughs, giggles, and smiles seem satisfying enough for everyone, at least thus far. The holiday season is young.

Uncle Ben stopped in well before dawn broke. It's still relatively quiet in Pilaf today, so we both enjoyed the peaceful conversation. We each sipped a cup of coffee while savoring a Giammalvo's Market apple fritter, and wondered if life in Pilaf was about to get as crazy as it was last Thanksgiving. When the first ray of sunlight pushed through the east window casting its yellow glow, Uncle Ben was driving away. Bailey's is quiet again, at least for now.

Monday, November 20, 2017, 3:55 PM

George dropped by after the lunch rush subsided. He was still on his mail route and stopped in for a moment to escape the brisk winds. His cheeks were pretty rosy, too. His holiday smile was wide. Don't ask me how I can tell the difference between his normal smile and his holiday smile, but I can. Perhaps it looks the same to someone who doesn't know him, so I'm assuming it's something discerned in the spirit. By December, the Christmas spring in his step is unmistakable. I find it a little odd that he hasn't offered even a hint of what he might do to freshen up his Christmas decorations this year.

Gracie has played a huge part in ordering inventory for the Thanksgiving and Christmas season over the last two weeks. She did an analysis of what was selling over the last ten years. Fortunately, Frank Bailey kept meticulous records that made the task interesting for her. One of the fascinating patterns has been with eggnog. If the autumnal weather pattern was near normal, eggnog sales were high. If November was warmer than normal, eggnog sales were slow. If November was cold and snowy, eggnog sales did poorly as well. Thus far, Stormy Windham's long range forecast for a near-normal November has been spot on. As Gracie predicted, we had a hard time keeping eggnog in stock.

Joel and Jessie stopped by Bailey's after school today. They both had that holiday skip in their step. A few of their friends joined them, so I treated them all to a small cup of hot chocolate. Their cheeks, as cherry red as they were, looked as though they needed a little warming up. It has been sunny all day, but quite crisp. It was tolerable this morning when wind was not an issue, but now we're seeing frequent gusts to 30 m.p.h. on my Bailey's weather station.

Both Joel and Jessie have great classmates. Most of them have been together since kindergarten. It's clear they all like one another, and as far as I can tell from their conversation, there are no favorites in the group. In fact, the group seems to function as a unit. When Jesus told us to love one another, He wasn't telling us to do something that was impossible. His command is so simple, that a group of 7th and 10th graders were effortlessly showing everyone in Pilaf how to get along. Indeed, our coming King's yoke is easy.

Tuesday, November 21, 2017, 8:55 AM

Ever since our early November snowfall, the month has been quite stable and nothing out of the ordinary for November. The beginning of the month had us all wondering if we were in for a classic winter. Even though Stormy did warn us about the likelihood of waking up to snow cover back on November 3rd, it still surprised quite a few people that Friday morning. Most of Bailey's early visitors couldn't stop talking about the "surprise snowfall." No matter how many times I reminded everyone that it was not a surprise snowfall and how Stormy warned us about it the day before, most everyone still called it a surprise. The only two people who did not play along were Uncle Ben and J. R. More than that, each saw great beauty in the early, wet snowfall. They both knew that it would all disappear within a few hours.

The morning was as still as could be. The stars were bright, not having to compete with any moonlight. At 28°F and no wind, I decided to walk to Bailey's. A flashlight had to be my companion since it was still quite dark when I began my walk. The one thing I noticed almost immediately was the stark difference in the sound of the morning now compared to a few months ago. The last time I walked to Bailey's, I barely needed a jacket and the birds were singing a September symphony in the bright, newly-risen sunlight. Today it's cold, very dark, and so quiet that I could hear Neil and Dawn's dog barking at some probable pre-sunrise critter over a half-mile away. Each season is just the right length. I realized how well I could see the beauty of every one. I love the variety. Living in the mundanely stable climate of Quito, Ecuador or San Diego, California would definitely not be my cup of tea.

I was tempted to take a short detour and walk past George's house, but thought better of the idea after remembering I had a flashlight that may attract attention from someone like Officer Caputo. I simply need to stay above any reproach brought on by innocent curiosity.

Speaking of George, he stopped in this morning and had coffee and a Danish with Uncle Ben. Usually, they would casually chat at the lunch counter. Today, their meeting appeared to be coordinated at a table for two in one of Bailey's tucked-away corners. They were looking something over, but it was too far away to identify. As curious as I was, I respected their space and kept busy at the counter and in the office. After George left, Uncle Ben stopped by the lunch counter to say hello, but that was it. No reference was made to the seemingly covert morning meeting with George. Very strange.

Tuesday, November 21, 2017, 4:28 PM

It has been more than a year since John Rowe made Pilaf his hometown. At the time, none of us were sure just what to expect. Everyone was certainly excited to have a celebrity living in our midst, but like that little pile of Brussel sprouts on an otherwise beautiful dinner presentation, there was a small portion of apprehension. We wondered if the peaceful pace of life was going to accelerate to a speed which none of us would find comfortable. Some of us had nightmares that we would one day wake up to find that Pilaf had grown to a busy metropolis with television executives running the town. No such thing ever happened. Pilaf is still the same wonderful town. The only difference is that John Rowe and his wife have now become a part of that deliberate, peaceful pace as though they had been Pilafians for decades. Certainly, there have been a few visitors drawn to our town to see if they could catch a glimpse of John or simply to see why he was drawn here. Virtually all of them have been kind and seem to appreciate our charm. On a few occasions, those visitors ran into John right here at Bailey's. John treated them to the same Pilaf allure that any of us would have extended.

He stopped in the store this afternoon just as Joel and Jessie raced in from the end of their school day. It was fun to see them greet John in the same fashion as Uncle Ben, George, or Jimmy Giammalvo. As we learned from John, that's exactly why he wanted to get away from the crazy pace of New York City. That's also why he seamlessly plugged into the gentle flow of life here.

Mrs. Krumm stopped in only minutes behind John, Joel, and Jessie. As usual, she did not say too much until John cornered her on the way out when she brought her items to the checkout counter. John was particularly interested in her assortment of items. She just looked at John and smiled. I pulled his arm just enough to get him to lean over in my direction.

"We don't ask Mrs. Krumm about her items, especially when they are unusual. It's a long story. I'll clue you in later."

John took my cue and steered the conversation in another direction.

A few more teachers from the school stopped by. That included Miss Marcie and Mr. Rayburn. Those are the names they've been using for each other ever since last Thanksgiving when they were married. Calling them Marcie and Arborio (Arbie for short) didn't feel right. Marcie did not like Miss Miller. She was delighted and proud to be a Rayburn. Finally, just after the first of the year, they started using Miss Marcie and Mr. Rayburn. It sounded right.

Everyone was mentioning how they were ready for the holidays as well as the church potluck on

Friday to celebrate the Rayburns first anniversary, Annie's 6th birthday, and the start of the Christmas season.

Wednesday, November 22, 2017, 9:00 AM

Bailey's was non-stop, controlled mayhem this morning. My goodness. Thanksgiving is tomorrow! How did that happen? Gracie's attention to detail saved me. Ordering a little extra eggnog was a good thing this year. We are down to three jars after a half-dozen more went out the door during the morning breakfast rush. Jessica just texted and asked me to bring one home, so I effectively have two that will likely be sold before I close early this afternoon.

George was in this morning, suited up to battle the cold breeze for his round of post office deliveries. At least he hasn't had a lot of snow to slow him down, that is up to now. Stormy's morning forecasts were hinting at a stormier pattern a little after

Thanksgiving. That will give everyone traveling for the holiday time to return before things get wintry.

Uncle Ben had another rendezvous with George this morning, this time without any papers. They chatted for a few minutes before having coffee and a doughnut, this time at the counter. At an opportune moment, I went over to freshen up their coffee mugs and casually asked them what kind of mischief they were planning. Both grinned. George was silent. Uncle Ben finally said, "Oh... you'll see."

At that exact moment, as if on cue, Officer Caputo walked in and came straight to the counter. Without missing a beat, he leaned in to the three of us and quietly announced that he was beefing up patrols around George's house this year until his Christmas decorations were operational. Even after staying far away from George's house until he turned on his display last year, I'm still paying the price of being in the wrong place at the wrong time several years ago.

Certainly, the interesting partnership between George and Uncle Ben has piqued my attention. It must have something to do with this year's display, but what else could George possibly add? Recent years' additions have included wireless, stereo speakers, and a giant snowman bubble at the post office. Yet, every year, he keeps outdoing himself.

Gracie is traveling to Gnadenhutten to spend Thanksgiving with family, so I've insisted she head out no later than noon to avoid driving at night.

Wednesday, November 22, 2017, 2:57 PM

Flurries have been intermittently in the air all afternoon. Nothing serious, but it does make me want to whistle something Christmasy.

Before lunch, and before Gracie left for the day, I took a short walk past George's place. I simply couldn't stand the suspense. While I did not dare climb up the front stairs and onto his front porch, I saw nothing out of the ordinary. George's lights were dutifully and meticulously hung. The wireless, outdoor speakers were mounted. That was it. I saw nothing new, that is except a hole in the ground near the sidewalk. It looked as if it had been dug with a post-hole digger. There was nothing in it. I didn't linger too long remembering Officer Caputo's tongue-in-cheek ribbing earlier today.

I just locked the front door. It's something I do every day out of routine. I don't think about it all that much on most days, but there is something magical about doing it a few minutes before 3 o'clock. There's a kind of giddiness reminiscent of my childhood days that anticipates the joy of a holiday. There are still sunny splashes squeezing in between the afternoon flurries, yet the street is as quiet as mid-evening. Everyone in Pilaf loves hanging out in their homes with family and friends on the eve of any holiday. That's why I close at 3 o'clock. It's why Giammalvo's Market closes at the same time. I can't think of any business that stays open much past 4 o'clock. If they do, their owners would be pretty lonely. It's interesting that one of the quietest places in all of Pilaf, the library, closes up at noon on the eve of Thanksgiving.

Joel and Jessie were done with school a few hours ago, right after lunch. They must have gone straight home. Some of the teachers came in for a couple of last minute items. The Pilaf lovebirds, Mr. Rayburn and Miss Marcie, were among them. They purchased the last bottle of eggnog. Gracie must have sold the other one before she left for Gnadenhutten. The last customer to leave today was Harry Buser. He initially came in looking for George, but ended up staying for a while, enjoying the company of anyone who was coming in for a late lunch or for last minute Thanksgiving items. He doesn't swing by all that often, so it was a treat to see him with that unmistakable holiday spirit.

Tomorrow's big annual football game between Pilaf and Borger is back at Borger this year. The Rayburns will have to wait for their second wedding anniversary to celebrate on the football field in Pilaf since we alternate fields every year. There was so much activity going on with the big halftime wedding that few people remember the football score, halftime or final. I do, but only because the total matched the kid's CLIP number: 17. Pilaf lost to Borger 10-7, but given the added festivities, you would have thought Pilaf won the NFL Super Bowl.

Speaking of Joel and Jessie's CLIP number, I've not seen it posted anywhere yet. It has been fun watching it over the last couple of years. I wonder if they've outgrown it? I hope not.

Thanksgiving Day, November 23, 2017, 7:07 AM

Thanksgiving Day is one day that Jennifer is up long before me. I have to be the most blessed man in the world on Thanksgiving. The scents that tickle my nose as I stir from my slumber are nothing short of sensory overload. It's a symphony of biscuits, bacon, eggs, turkey, gravy, bread, and apple pie. Ah, yes. Apple pie. While I'm certain Miss Marcie's apple pie is excellent, Jennifer's "Mount Mansfield" pie is the one to beat, in my humble opinion. I've yet to convince Jennifer that having her apple pie with coffee on Thanksgiving morning would make the perfect breakfast before heading out to the annual football game. I already made my appeal this morning. The result was no different. One of these years, I'll simply have to sneak a piece and blame it on Bonnie and Clyde.

Speaking of Bonnie and Clyde, I haven't seen much of them in the last few months. I've seen them high in transit every once in awhile, but not at Bailey's. I haven't heard George or Uncle Ben talk about them either. Perhaps they are making life interesting for our neighbors in Borger.

The house is not only filled with phenomenal scents right now, but it's also unusually warm and even somewhat humid in the kitchen. So much so, that it never dawned on me that it was likely very cold, just as Stormy predicted yesterday. Not until moments ago did I look at Jennifer's kitchen window thermometer. I stared in disbelief. How can it be that cold when we are dancing around a kitchen that gives us the impression that we live in a semi-tropical climate? It's 11°F! That's the coldest Thanksgiving I remember in a very long time. If you look at the traditional liquid-in-tube thermometer from an angle above it, it looks like 12°F or 13°F. Granted, while there isn't much difference, 12°F or 13°F simply sounds better than 11°F. Yesterday's flurries persisted through the night to greet us with a very thin dusting of granular snow. The tree limbs are moving a little, suggesting that low wind chills will do everything it can to rob us of our warmth at the game. We've been through that drill before. Thank goodness for advances in thermal apparel.

Thanksgiving Day, November 23, 2017, 8:00 PM

It seems like there's always something unique and memorable that characterizes the annual Thanksgiving Day football game between our Pilaf Warriors and the Borger Bulldogs. After last year's memorable, last-play, last-second loss here in Pilaf, the other side of the coin showed up this year in Borger. It was scoreless at the end of regulation time. The referees were staying warmer than the players as they ran around throwing one penalty flag after another. After a while, it was more entertaining watching the referees than the very slow and highly defensive game.

The halftime band performances were the highlight of this year's game. The reason for that was the special performance that honored the Rayburns who will celebrate their first anniversary tomorrow. For the Borger band's last number, an anniversary love song, the band threw protocol out the window as they turned around to face the opponent's side to serenade our celebrated couple sitting at mid-field near the top of the bleachers. If there had been a "kiss-cam," it would have been waiting for the teacher and principal to smooch for all the students to see. Thankfully for them, their classy peck was not on a jumbotron.

Our Warriors prevailed in double-overtime, 6-0. But by then, more than half of the crowd had filed out of the stadium. Everyone was cold to the core and the final score was a mere postscript, even for the players. On paper, it was a win for Pilaf. In the player's hearts, it was an evenly matched tie with both teams congratulating each other on another great rival game.

For John and Eloise Rowe, it was their second time attending this Thanksgiving Day tradition. They don't really remember their first game all that well since everyone in Pilaf made a big fuss over their attendance. It wasn't that Pilaf was star-struck as much as it was the desire to ensure they were welcomed and embraced as Pilafians. So many people came up to chat with them that they missed most of the game. They also missed every key play that contributed to Pilaf's decisive win over the Bulldogs last year. About the only thing they remember with any sort of clarity is the big halftime wedding. All eyes were on the beautiful Miss Marcie and the dashing Mr. Rayburn, joined at the fifty-yard line by our pastor, Dr. O'Connor.

Back in the warmth of our home, Jennifer's meal was truly outstanding. How is it that each Thanksgiving keeps getting better and better? Her Mount Mansfield apple pie was as good as ever. There was the added twist of the bourbon-brown sugar sauce glazed over the vanilla ice cream from Rich's Dairy Farm. It was a perfectly placed exclamation point on the entire day.

Friday, November 24, 2017, 9:57 AM

It's another frigid morning, but at least this one is clear and still. The deep chill can actually be enjoyable without the air in motion. The stars were brilliant in the moonless, pre-twilight sky. As the subtle dawn colors chased away the night, the delicate layers of blue wood smoke added a serene look against the landscape during my drive to Bailey's. The "morning star" Venus is now sinking quickly in the eastern sky, diving faster and faster into brighter dawn. It's pretty low as dawn breaks. It was the high and mighty, exceedingly bright morning star all summer and autumn. According to George, Venus will be too close to the sun to be visible as we approach Christmas. The good news is that it will become a brilliant sunset object as we navigate into 2018, staying in the evening sky through much of the year.

Compared to previous years, the customer flow was essentially the same this morning as in the past. Still feeling stuffed from the wonders of the Thanksgiving feast, people usually come in only for a cup of tea or coffee. Even if I flew in the tastiest apple fritters from Miss Kay's Sweet Treats in Louisiana (something I arrange for special occasions), I suspect a family of four would be happy to split one while still digesting yesterday's huge dinner. I digress.

The cinnamon buns and cherry Danish that I did order from Giammalvo's for this morning were gobbled up an hour ago! I would have never guessed that. I wonder if the very cold morning air had anything to do with the robust post-holiday appetites. I'll have to ask Gracie to do her research magic. I know she'll have fun with that one.

John and Eloise Rowe stopped in this morning and mingled with everyone. They apparently spent Thanksgiving with their son in Cincinnati, driving back late last night. They were not about to miss the celebration they arranged for the Rayburns tonight at the church fellowship hall. Both John and Eloise will be busy making a dessert reception. So many people wanted to come that having an open house at their Victorian home would be challenging. It was Dr. O'Connor who suggested moving the anniversary celebration to fellowship hall.

I hope the Andersons stop by with Annie today. I borrowed a couple of George's CDs from his extensive Christmas collection to fill Bailey's with the kind of Christmas music I like. That's not to say there are Christmas songs I don't like. I like them all, however, sometimes the playlists on some of the stations that offer 24-hour holiday music doesn't strike my Christmas bell squarely. According to Annie, Christmas music should never be played or intentionally enjoyed until after her birthday is over. But now that it's the day after Thanksgiving, how can I not welcome the Christmas season? Surely it will be acceptable once Annie hears her favorite Christmas CD on my Bailey's playlist.

Friday, November 24, 2017, 9:55 PM

Could the day after Thanksgiving possibly be as exciting as the holiday itself? Usually, this day is rather anticlimactic, but Bailey's was busier than normal. In addition to running out of breakfast pastries before 9 o'clock, we sold out of Gracie's corn chowder before the lunch rush was over. Corn chowder is one of those things that cannot be made quickly when your supply runs out. Sure, one could open up a few cans of corn chowder and heat it up quickly, but compared to Gracie's slow-cooked chowder, it would be like comparing cream cheese stuffed French crêpes with stale, burnt toast. We don't serve stale, burnt toast. I still remember my grandmother telling me that eating burnt toast would make me sing like a pro. I wonder how that old wive's tale started? My grandmother believed it. Not me. I tried it. Burnt toast makes me cough. A lot.

At every turn and during every hour, there was chatter about tonight's dessert anniversary reception at the church. Everyone wondered what John and Eloise were going to make. How often does a nationally known chef invite an entire town to a personally catered dessert reception? The only request for entry was an anniversary gift for the couple.

Even on this cold November night, the church fellowship hall did not take long to warm up with all the people arriving. When the guests of honor arrived, they were escorted to the head of the large, round table. Jennifer and I had the honor of being seated beside them, along with Annie Anderson and her family. Everyone else was instructed to grab any seat at any other table. As disorganized as that may sound, everyone found a table and was seated in less than a minute. I guess when John Rowe tells you to grab a seat, you don't waste any time!

David Russell, who normally plays his violin at church, emerged from the kitchen with his instrument and began to play. The strolling serenade captivated everyone. When David concluded, the entire room stood on its feet with a thunderous applause. Right on cue, John and Eloise opened the main kitchen doors to reveal tonight's dessert as it rolled out on the first cart. They were apple tarts in the shape of an apple with a bright, apple red glaze. John matched the color of the candle that Annie Anderson unconsciously moved at Pilaf's big apple pie baking contest. Brilliant!

As the crowd was finishing, John emerged from the kitchen with a special birthday cake for Annie. I've never seen a cake that looked like a giant apple! He also had a small gift in his hand which he gave to her. The room began to quiet as all eyes moved to Annie's table. After blowing out the single candle on the cake, she opened what appeared to be a music CD. Annie held it up high with a big smile. It was Ace Molar's brand new Christmas CD. John must have connections, because the long-anticipated release date isn't until tomorrow. It was now Annie's official duty to start the Christmas season in Pilaf by playing her new CD for everyone to enjoy.

Saturday, November 25, 2017, 7:44 AM

Hugs are an essential expression of endearment, love, and kindness. There's a famous family therapist, Virginia Satir, who said, "We need four hugs a day for survival, eight hugs a day for maintenance, and twelve hugs a day for growth." I'll go for a dozen or more every day, every time. Both

Joel and Jessie gave me long, tight hugs before I left for Bailey's this morning. This was especially sweet since it was obvious that both had just awakened to this new day. It was the first thing they did after coming down the stairs. I'm glad that Jennifer and I were always liberal with hugs, to each other, our children, and all of our friends. It's passing on a tradition that was passed on to us. I love recalling the wonderful hugs from my mother and father. I miss them terribly. Until I get my hugs when I see them in eternity, and I know I will, it's my turn to pass it on to the next generation (and eventually two).

Our weather continues to be quiet. The air is no longer bitter cold and the crusty coating of snow that greeted us as dawn broke on Thanksgiving morning has long since sublimated. While it's not bitter cold, it certainly isn't warm, either. I stoked a nice fire in the woodstove upon arriving at the store. It has already been visited several times this morning before customers worked their way to the counter for coffee and a breakfast goodie.

George was the first to stop by this morning; yes even before Uncle Ben. When Uncle Ben did show up a little after George, I was able to rib him about having his title as my loyal first daily customer stripped away by a postal carrier. Uncle Ben smiled, but you could tell he didn't like that thought. He promised to "fix" that. When George left, he did take

Uncle Ben with him. They're up to something. I just know it.

Saturday, November 25, 2017, 5:11 PM

I relish these quiet moments after locking Bailey's front door and pulling the blinds. When I worked in the city, I did everything I could to bolt out the door when the work day was done. I expedited things by putting everything except my briefcase in the car during my last hour of labor. It's nothing like that now. Even if it's only 5-10 minutes after I close Bailey's for the day, I take the time to marvel at God's goodness to me. It's not hard to do. He brought me back home.

It's raining lightly now. I had hoped the precipitation would hold off until later tonight. I wanted to convince the family to walk by George's house. Officer Caputo has nothing on me this year. No sneak peeks. Walking past his house doesn't count, even walking slowly. Anyone can do that at any time of the day or night.

Leading the Sunday morning Bible study before worship services on Sunday morning has been a delightful stretch for me. While I read God's Word every day, there is an extra element of gravity when you have to then lead a meaningful study. We've been working through the Epistle to the Ephesians. It's a lofty, amazing book, telling us who we really are in Christ. Not wanting to miss any and all of its richness, my pace has been deliberate. I hope it's only my imagination, but I sense a little restlessness in the class.

Sunday, November 26, 2017, 6:38 AM

Up a little early this morning to spend some time in the passage in Ephesians we will focus on today in the Bible study class. I'm expecting a good crowd, not because I'm leading it or because we are in Ephesians, but because Jennifer made some homemade chocolate croissants to share. I made sure to spread the word at the store yesterday. Everyone who has tasted them raves over their buttery, chocolaty goodness. Food for the body always helps the absorption of food for the soul. Even Jesus fed the thousands who came to hear Him speak truth.

It's still dark outside, but I can tell that Pilaf is wrapped in a light fog this morning. The deck is wet and I can't see much past a half mile. Nothing is frozen, though. It's 41 °F. Freezing fog is never fun. It's deceptive. Freezing fog has an identical look and feel to the unfrozen variety, so venturing out for any reason without exercising extra caution will often have disastrous results. That thin layer of ice masquerading as a wet layer has taken more than its fair share of Pilaf's ankles and other limbs. Doc Fairbanks can attest to this.

We never did have the chance to drive past George's house yet. The light rain didn't stop last night until we all decided to jump into our pajamas, make popcorn, and pull out a Christmas movie before bedtime. Jessie insisted on the claymation classic, Rudolph The Red-Nosed-Reindeer. Knowing that Jessie would pick that flick, Joel mouthed the words silently in nearly perfect sync when Jessie made her choice known. In fact, if no other Christmas film existed, it would be all right with Jessie.

Sunday, November 26, 2017, 4:22 PM

I'm glad I unplugged from the football grid. My interest is casual, hoping to see the Browns play the kind of football that is fun to watch. Instead, it's more of the same. They lost to the Bengals with eight seconds remaining in the game. I'm tempted to cheer for the New England Patriots just to see what it's like to back a winning team again, but Joel tells me that it's "illegal" to back a team that gets a kick out of deflating footballs. At least the Browns are doing better than last year. Anything is an improvement over last year's near winless record, I suppose.

Watching habits have changed over the last few decades. I remember watching football on Sunday afternoons with much more enthusiasm. Even though the game hasn't changed much over the decades, interest has. Jennifer and I think the internet, on-demand culture has pushed the audience to expect faster-paced games. Precisely why we no longer see the Pro-Bowler's Tour on ABC every Saturday afternoon. This nationally televised bowling tournament held our attention then, but it became "too slow" to watch in recent decades, even though the pace of the game itself hadn't changed. Over twenty years has passed since that final weekly broadcast. I miss seeing it. I wonder if football will follow the same pathway? Or will the game and the way it airs change to cater to an audience that demands something different? Interesting to ponder, but only as an outsider. That's exactly why unplugging was the best thing our family has done.

Aside from a few short, interesting weather episodes, November has been fairly quiet and delightfully normal this year. I walked to the edge of the Jasmine Creek footpath this afternoon. My jacket and hat were both almost too warm. Thank goodness for zippers. Stormy Windham hinted at long-term changes for December. I hope he elaborates tomorrow morning. My favorite month starts on Friday.

Monday, November 27, 2017, 7:12 AM

Uncle Ben stopped by Bailey's quite early today. I don't think it was three minutes after I unlocked the front door that he came waltzing in. I anticipated his need before he even asked and pulled out a cherry Danish, one of his favorites. I was right. Uncle Ben has a certain joyful gait when he's in the mood for his favorite morning treat. When I first started running Bailey's, I would make a game of guessing what he might ask for. He delightfully played along. I got it wrong most of the time, but after a while, I started picking up on certain nuances. It's actually a skill I picked up from Joel while he was growing up. Joel's powers of observations were amazing, even as an infant. When you thought his facial grimace meant something was wrong, we learned he was actually paying very close attention to the details of what was happening around him.

We spoke a little about Sunday's Bible study. He shared some interesting things about the passage in Ephesians Chapter 5. My Bible was open on the counter near my coffee mug as steamed curled up in beautiful patterns. We both agreed that the arrangement would make a great photo. Uncle Ben read my mind when he talked about how the coffee's steam is so dynamic, just like God's Word. It's as irresistible and captivating as watching the steam rise from the coffee mug.

He told me that he already started spending time in the next passage of Ephesians for the following Sunday. That was refreshing to hear. I say that because the majority of our Sunday morning class admitted that they did not carefully read the passage for discussion. That limits the depth to which we can go as a group. One group is ready to dig deeply. The other group shows up with a trowel in hand, but it's still as clean as a whistle and the soil is unbroken, sometimes even hard and crusty. I do what I can to encourage preparing for our time together. The old adage is true. You can lead a horse to water, but you certainly cannot make it drink.

While it's easy to become discouraged, I must remain encouraged by people like Harry Buser. Two years ago, he saw no need to attend our Bible study group before worship services. His transformation has been nothing short amazing. In fact, I frequently hear him invite others to our group when he comes into the store. It's my prayer that everyone in our town taps into that zeal.

Monday, November 27, 2017, 4:44 PM

"32"

That apparently was the focus of some sidewalk art I stumbled across near John Rowe's Victorian home, just up the street from the store. I was on my way to mail a few Christmas cards that Jennifer asked me to bring to the post office after the lunch rush was done. I've never seen such amazing sidewalk art anywhere. The level of detail and the number of colors used was something to behold.

Around the number 32, there were gold stars, angelic halos, light bulbs, a dog, and a cat. I tried to make sense of it, but it seemed so random. As beautiful as it was, nothing connected including its placement near John and Eloise's home.

It looked like the Rowes were starting to decorate for Christmas. There were boxes of lights and an extension ladder leaning on the side of their home, but John wasn't visible when I walked by. I'm anxious to see how he decorates. He wasn't able to do much last year as they were still busy unpacking boxes and settling into the flow of life as Pilafians.

I dutifully mailed Jennifer's cards inside the post office. George was actually inside at the counter, taking care of a customer's box, when I walked in. We waved to each other, but I did not want to take his attention away from his customer, so I didn't stop to chat. After the letters were slipped into the mail chute, I donned my earmuffs and walked back to the store. I couldn't help thinking about why Jennifer specifically asked me to make sure that the cards went into the mail chute inside the post office, and not in the outdoor mailbox receptacle two blocks from the store. She said that she wanted to know, with absolute certainty, that the cards were on their way. I can't ever remember the post office's failure to deliver something that I placed in that outdoor receptacle, or any other for that matter. I find it interesting that there is an extra measure of assurance that a letter or card placed in the chute inside the post office will reach its destination with greater speed. I should invent a name for that, just like the sniglet once coined to describe the act of re-checking a mailbox a second time to make sure that a letter dropped in made it into the sack. That word invented by HBO's Rich Hall was "premblememblemation."

Tuesday, November 28, 2017, 8:17 AM

George stopped in just before heading to the post office. He asked me if I knew who drew the "32" on the sidewalk near John's house, or what it meant. He noticed it yesterday during his rounds. Despite being the place to ask such questions, neither I nor anyone else in Bailey's could answer either question. I tried to remind myself to ask Joel and Jessie if they were keeping track of their CLIP number like the last few years, but it slipped my mind when we all started talking about how we wanted to decorate for Christmas this year. It seems like 32 would be a feasible CLIP number for this date. They showed just as much interest in learning who the sidewalk chalk artist is. The artwork is stunning. Both Joel and Jessie love to doodle, but this was definitely not their work.

The artwork may not last long. Stormy talked about rain moving in this afternoon and tonight. He mentioned a pattern shift that would greet us soon after we flipped our calendars to December. All of the kids in Pilaf have been anxious for something a little more than flurries, yet they all seem to be exercising a great deal patience with the atmosphere.

Tuesday, November 28, 2017, 10:11 PM

Both kids seem to have an unusual amount of homework since Thanksgiving break ended. Jennifer told me they were quite busy upon arriving home, taking only minor breaks until I arrived home after closing Bailey's. During a phenomenal chicken pot pie dinner, we discovered that both had homework assignments in each subject. On top of that, each has a major test on Friday. For Joel it's history. For Jessie, it's math. As much as they enjoy some leisure time after dinner, it was clear that each was focused on returning to their studies after a light dessert of vanilla ice cream topped with an assortment of berries.

Ice cream is good anytime of year. It may be served a bit more frequently in the summer, but the chilly breezes of late autumn will never persuade me otherwise if I am in the mood for ice cream. All you have to do is to look to Alaska's consumption of ice cream. Alaska shares the highest annual per capita consumption of ice cream with Rhode Island, another northern state. There is even an ice cream manufacturer in Fairbanks that operates year round. I can't imagine that any community bathed in -40°F temperatures has any desire for ice cream, but it does. Perhaps a bowl of ice cream with world leaders would have ended the "cold war" more quickly.

One of the subjects at the dinner table was decorating for Christmas. I knew this would be a great way to help the kids temporarily break mental suction with their pending school work. Jennifer and I now had their undivided attention. Joel wanted to go high tech again, especially outside. Jessie wanted to go simple and elegant. Jennifer suggested a blend of both. This was the peaceful solution. I would tackle the outside with Joel. Jennifer would tackle the inside with Jessie. We are setting Saturday aside to, at the very least, begin the process.

Wednesday, November 29, 2017, 7:55 AM

I woke to the sound of very heavy rain this morning. The sound of rain is generally a peaceful affair. I wish I could say that about this one. Sammy is usually eager to jump on my lap during my morning wake-up routine, but he was noticeably absent. I called him, but saw no trace of him. Despite being unusually loud, there was still something peacefully rhythmic in the rainfall's beatdown. I'm assuming it was enough of an atmospheric lullaby to keep Jennifer, Joel, and Jessie sound asleep right up to the time I left for Bailey's.

George stopped in a little bit ago. His rain poncho has so much water on it that he glistened like a Christmas tree. Perhaps this Christmas we ought to keep George sprayed down with water, standing under one of our lights by the front door. Despite knowing that he would be battling to stay dry on his upcoming route delivery, his smile was wide and genuine. There's something about a good old-fashioned rainstorm that gives George an added sense of pride in his work. George personifies the unofficial postal carrier's creed found in large, block lettering on the post office building in New York City: "Neither snow nor rain nor heat nor gloom of night stays these couriers from the swift completion of their appointed rounds." Give George a beautiful, sunny day and he is joyful. Give George a rainy day like this and he is no less joyful. It's no wonder he is so popular whether he is on his route or just hanging out at Bailey's.

We talked about the rain and how we could not remember the last time we had such a long lasting gulley-washer. It may be a few years. We also both wondered if the sidewalk chalk artwork just outside John Rowe's would be washed away. That's very likely. I wonder if anyone had the forethought to snap a photo on their smartphone? I had mine when I came across the vibrant work, but that thought never crossed my mind. My guess is that it would have been Joel and Jessie's first or second thought.

It seems like everyone who has seen it is hoping more shows up despite the quizzical who and why. Come to think of it, I think I'm in the same camp.

Wednesday, November 29, 2017, 3:39 PM

I wish more people had their Christmas decorations up and on today. It was dark all day, so dark that one could easily see any outdoor lights that were illuminated even at noon. At least the heavy rain is gone, replaced by drizzle and fog. My weather station shows almost two inches of rain. If the drizzle is persistent, my guess is we will see two inches or over by the time I head home.

Today's lunch chatter included news of the sidewalk chalk art that mysteriously appeared on Monday. Apparently George and I were far from the only people interested in seeing if the artwork had survived the rainstorm. Everyone I spoke to said that it was totally gone. I simply had to see it for myself, so I took the short walk to John's house about an hour ago while Gracie minded the store. Sure enough, there wasn't a trace of the beautiful work of art.

Thursday, November 30, 2017, 7:20 AM

The sky is assuring us of a much quieter day despite the standing water still lurking in various low spots. I noticed that some of the shallower pools in Bailey's parking lot had a few icy feathers hugging the outside edges. My weather station reads 30°F. Stormy is still spinning a tale of weather changes in the next few days. Pilaf has long been ready for some weather action. November has been, well, down right boring.

Just before dinner last night, Jessie showed me some of the artwork she made during art class. Her focus is yet another indication that Pilaf is ready for any kind of weather change. It was a landscape filled with all kinds of interesting weather. I'm glad she was anxious to explain it since the landscape included snow, blowing snow, freezing rain, rain, and a rainbow, all falling on different parts of the landscape. While such a scene would surely be a nightmare for Stormy to forecast, the many microclimates squeezed onto one sheet was surely something captivating to anyone's imagination, particularly Jessie's.

Seeing the artwork made me realize I failed to ask either Jessie or Joel if they were keeping track of the CLIP number this year, and if it was "32." I kept that question for casual dinnertime conversation. When I introduced the topic, both of them smiled. They were pleased that I remembered a tradition that started several years ago. Since I did not see any number prominently displayed anywhere in their rooms, I thought perhaps they had outgrown the tradition and allowed it to start the fermentation process that would allow the CLIP number to develop into a fine memory.

"We will be keeping track of the CLIP number," Jessie proudly exclaimed, "but we decided to officially wait until December first."

Hmmmm. That's Friday. When I asked them if the CLIP number could have been "32" earlier in the week, they said it was possible, but counting anything before December 1 wouldn't be official. They could not remember if they might have shared any number, much less "32" with anyone.

Thursday, November 30, 2017, 8:01 PM

Officer Caputo stopped in for lunch today. He's always quick to offer a friendly smile and a new joke to anyone who looks just a little too serious. Usually it happens to others. Today, it was my turn. Perhaps I've been trying to play it too straight since just before Thanksgiving, trying to stay away from George's display until he was ready to unveil it.

After the Christmas joke with a really bad pun for the punch line, he asked me why I haven't been by to see George's new addition to his Christmas display. I almost said something about having walked by his house about a week ago, but I caught myself and simply shrugged my shoulders. No sooner did I start to steer the conversation in a different direction, George walked in. His timing was suspiciously fortuitous.

"When will you and your family be stopping by my house for a Christmas visit? I haven't seen you yet!"

I promised him that I had set aside Friday evening to scoop up my family and stroll down for a visit. Both he and Officer Caputo chuckled when I told George that I would not leave without getting some figgy pudding. I haven't the foggiest idea what figgy pudding is.

Friday, December 1, 2017, 9:10 AM

I love Fridays. I love flipping my giant, old-fashioned calendar from November to December. I especially enjoy it when the two coincide. It doesn't happen all that often! The most recent time before today was in 2006. Joel was a 4-year-old toddler and Jessie was still a little baby. The next one won't occur until 2023. Joel will probably be a college junior and Jessie graduating from Pilaf High School. Yikes. I'm glad I have six years to get accustomed to thinking about my youngest as a high school graduate.

Stormy just delivered his outlook for December on WPLF-FM, something he traditionally does on the first day of the month. It sounds like a quirky month ahead beginning with a storm that arrives late tonight. Rain first, then snow tomorrow. We've yet to see more than a candy coating of snow. It would be appropriate given that "meteorological winter" began about nine hours ago. Since the winter solstice floats in a three-day margin from year to year, Stormy says that it's difficult to use the astronomical marker for weather bookkeeping. It does make more sense to welcome winter on December 1.

Friday, December 1, 2017, 11:11 PM

It has been a long, full day, but the house is now quieting down after an evening of activity. Joel and Jessie are still exchanging giggles from their open bedroom doors. Each giggle or chatter is quickly becoming less frequent. I suspect by the time I finish my post, the house will be quiet aside from the delicate sound of Jennifer sipping herbal tea and the cold, windy rain that began falling about an hour ago.

Thankfully, despite threatening skies, the clouds remained unproductive late this afternoon and early evening, but the winds were freshening. It went along with my weather station at Bailey's showing a rapidly falling barometer. Stormy's afternoon weather update was spot-on.

I hope we see him sometime this Christmas season. If he does wander through, it will be the fourth consecutive December he has paid us a visit. I still remember the first time when he was near George's house looking at his Christmas lights. Even in his leisure time, he went into his familiar teaching mode, telling us why sound travels easier when the air is cold. My guess is that he would not make the forty-minute drive into Pilaf tonight given the impending storm. It would be fun if he simply moved here as a permanent resident. We would have not one, but two celebrities in our midst!

Jennifer made a casserole she hasn't made in years tonight. It was Marzetti, a skillet dish with noodles, tomato soup, cheese, and ground beef. I almost forgot how tasty it was. The kids raved over it and want this dish to be added to our meal rotation. Fine by me!

After dinner, we all piled into the car to drive around the gazebo in the center of town. The decorations were outstanding, as usual. After parking the car, we all hiked down to George's house to see his decorations. Was there a new display, color scheme, or giant inflatable this year? Whatever it was, he was anxious for me to discover it.

As we approached his house, we heard some new Christmas music that initially didn't sound familiar. As we drew closer, I recognized it as the song, We Need A Little Christmas, coming from his outdoor speakers, but it was not the version by Percy Faith I've come to know and love. This one had a heavy rhythm and blues sound, a most unusual musical flavor for George.

A quick glance seemed to indicate that there was nothing new to George's decorations. Was it his choice of music that was the highlight? That didn't make any sense and did not match George's hype during the week. Not until I was about three house lengths away did I finally see something new. At first it looked like a fancy birdhouse. But the house portion was too large and too close to eye level.

While Jennifer and the kids walked onto George's front porch for a closer look at his lights, and with nobody else around, I walked up to the box. There were plexiglass doors in front, but the reflection from George's lights made it impossible to know what was inside, if anything. Assuming the doors were an invitation for passers-by to open the box, I opened both of them simultaneously. It revealed two stacked shelves containing what appeared to be music CDs and a sign that said, "Take One or Leave One to Share."

"I've been waiting for you," a low, breathy voice exclaimed inches from my ear. It was Officer Caputo. He nearly sent me to the moon and back! Didn't I look in every direction before opening those doors? I'm beginning to think he has powers to materialize out of thin air like Barbara Eden did in the 1960s sitcom, I Dream Of Jeannie.

"Don't worry, you're supposed to open those doors," he continued. It was the music equivalent of a little free library where people take and leave, in this case, a music CD. I examined a few of them and realized that every CD in the box was a Christmas CD. That's what Uncle Ben must have been building for George. His craftsmanship was all over the box. It also just dawned on me that this is exactly where I discovered the post hole in front of George's house about a week and a half ago.

George came out to the porch and gave us all a cup of hot cider. I complimented George that he had outdone himself yet again. It was great seeing what I call "that mailman smile." George went on to encourage me to take a few of the CDs since my Christmas playlist at Bailey's was becoming too predictable.

We returned to the car rather late, having spent more than half of our time on George's porch, so I resisted Joel and Jessie's request for an official CLIP run. Joel and Jessie persisted. Since it was, in fact, December 1st, getting the first official count should not be postponed. Jennifer chimed in and added to the kids' defense by reminding me that it wasn't a school homework night. I could not help smiling. With Gracie opening up Bailey's for me tomorrow morning, why not?

Tonight's CLIP number is 42.

Saturday, December 2, 2017, 8:55 AM

We must have all been so tired from Friday's activities, that we all slept through the atmospheric transition. It's unusual for Jennifer or me to sleep completely through the night anymore, but we did. Sleeping through the night for Joel and Jessie is something I imagine they will enjoy for at least a few decades. I'm glad I did not tell them that Stormy was forecasting a transition from rain to snow for today. That's as good as setting a pre-sunrise alarm clock for them. The kids are still sleeping. I told Jennifer that I would rouse them by 9 o'clock. Jennifer is going to try to save their reaction to the snow by filming their excitement on her smartphone.

The light coming from the bedroom window seemed particularly bright, but soft. Since no one set an alarm, I rolled over and saw 8:15 a.m. Bailey's was in good hands with Gracie in charge. At least I thought so until I looked out the window and saw far more snow than what Stormy predicted! The transition was supposed to take place around late-morning. I checked my phone and relaxed when I saw no messages from Gracie. I'll assume all is okay, and enjoy sipping my coffee with Sammy sitting contentedly on my lap watching winter's first real assault on Pilaf. Talk about great ambience to decorate for Christmas this afternoon.

I'll head in to Bailey's a little later for a few hours. I'm glad I took today as a casual day. My suspicion is that Joel and Jessie will want to do something with all that snow outside.

Saturday, December 2, 2017, 7:54 PM

I'm exhausted, but it's the good kind. Fortunately, Gracie had everything under control all day since I spent the entire morning building a snow castle with the kids. It looks especially good tonight since Joel suggested lighting it with some of the programmable LED flood lamps we used in the front yard last Christmas. If we were going to illuminate it, I suggested building it in the front yard where passers-by could see it. The other added advantage was having a grand view of the castle from the kitchen window as well as Joel and Jessie's bedrooms upstairs.

The snow was perfect for this kind of project. The six inches of snow was wet enough to hold its shape as we put the pieces of the castle together. It was snowing all morning, but the serious flakes that were doing the major accumulating stopped as we opened the back door to begin our project. We positioned the floodlights in places that we thought would give the castle the greatest visual depth, but we wouldn't know until dusk if we succeeded.

Lunch never tasted so good. Jennifer called us all inside for tomato bisque and grilled cheese sandwiches.

Since Joel was satisfied with the decorated castle for as long as it would last, he graciously offered to help Jessie decorate the inside any way she wanted.

Sammy cautiously watched from the kitchen as I unboxed the artificial tree. My guess is that he was making sure I was pulling out the same one we purchased last year. Having a much smaller three-foot tree is far less intimidating than the one that came crashing down on him several years ago. Call me crazy, but I thought I heard a sigh of relief as Sammy yawned.

I did briefly pop my head into Bailey's. It was more of a social visit than anything else. The clam chowder was gone. There wasn't much left of the minestrone soup either. It was a big soup day, not all that surprising given the snow and cold. I asked Gracie if John Rowe ever sampled her corn chowder? She didn't think so. I must arrange that. I truly think his distinguished culinary palate will be impressed.

I'm generally ready for Sunday morning's Bible class, but I'd like to go over the material once more. I'll have enough time tomorrow morning if I get up early enough before the house comes alive. If I tried reading tonight, I think my eyes would drop shut in minutes.

Sunday, December 3, 2017, 6:44 AM

Joel and Jessie will not be happy when they look out the window at our snow castle. It looks like a lumpy mound. The spires which were so meticulously illuminated with alternating red and green flood lights are now unrecognizable. I turned off the floodlights as it only accentuated the cruel prank the atmosphere played on our youth. Did it warm up so quickly while we slept? A check of Jennifer's outdoor thermometer outside the kitchen window verified my suspicion. It was 56°F. I must have tuned out of Stormy's forecast beyond the call for a Saturday snowfall. I'm glad we all took a few photos of the intricate castle yesterday.

Before opening my Bible and study materials, I stepped outside on the front steps for a moment. Doing so in my slippers was easy since the sidewalk to the front door landing was shoveled well the day before. The concrete was only a little moist. I was surprised by the stillness. With the air so mild after a day of cold and snow, I was almost expecting to hear the pre-sunrise symphony of birds calling the sun to rise above the eastern hills. The birds are smarter than me though. They're the ones in Florida, Louisiana, Mexico, and Brazil.

Sunday, December 3, 2017, 8:40 PM

December is an amazing month of bounty on so many different levels. One of them is our church where we had a full house today. It seemed like all of Pilaf was there. Dr. O'Connor preached an inspiring message on sharing and how we all have a greater capacity for this at Christmas. That was the compliment. The challenge was to practice that same attitude year round. He mentioned George's new little free music library as a great example of ways we can share with our neighbors.

Earlier this morning, Joel and Jessie were disappointed to see our work in the front yard reduced by a warm nighttime breeze. They quickly turned it around though by suggesting a walk down to the Jasmine Creek after church and lunch. With so much melting snow overnight, the creek was flowing fast. We stayed a comfortable distance from the drop-off, observing the current a safe distance from the trail's edge. With the trail being so slippery with mud and pockets of wet snow, visions of accidentally slipping into the cold, thigh-deep creek was not particularly appealing.

During the walk, I asked them what they learned in their Sunday school class. Without missing a beat, they both talked about reading your Bible every day, even if it's just a short passage. Then Joel asked me something that startled me.

"Dad, how come you read your Bible only once in a while?"

That stopped me, quite literally, in my tracks. Didn't he and Jessie know that I read my Bible every single day? My answer was gentle but swift. I do read my Bible every day. But now my curiosity drove me to ask them why they though I only read it every once in a while. I should have known the answer. Most of the time, I retreat to the kitchen in the quiet of the morning to open God's Word. Everyone is still sleeping. During the weekdays, I leave the house for Bailey's before the kids are up for school. While it's my goal to allow Christ to live through me in daily living, my family likely doesn't see me studying our Creator's manual for successful living on a daily basis.

Joel was perfectly satisfied with my answer and assurances of my daily study, but I must find ways for all of my family to actually witness my commitment to daily reading. After all, I am trying to find creative ways to encourage the Sunday morning Bible study class to feast on all the good that is in the Holy Scriptures.

The kids are now getting ready for bed. Sleep will come quickly. I can see it in their eyes. Perhaps they will dream about some of the Christmas decorations we've seen on our CLIP run. The weekend was a good one for decorating. The CLIP number has jumped to 59.

Monday, December 4, 2017, 7:00 AM

The snow from the weekend is already gone. Stormy made sure his audience knew that it would return, but not for a few days.

I keep a Bible at home in my study, and a Bible here at Bailey's. I left my home Bible open on the kitchen counter before I left for the store. It was turned to Psalm 16. I made use of the new electronic memo board I bought a few months ago to leave Joel and Jessie a note pointing out verse 8: "I keep my eyes always on the Lord. With Him at my right hand, I will not be shaken." How can we best do this? By staying in His Word. I think I'll deviate from the Sunday study in Ephesians and do a special study on the importance of daily reading.

Uncle Ben wandered in just as the coffee finished brewing. Perfect timing. It was still pretty quiet, and I was caught up on errands and paperwork, so I insisted on blessing him with coffee and a cherry Danish on the house. His smile was all I needed to see his gratitude.

I complimented him on the free music library he built and installed for George. He said they were inspired by John Rowe's little free library in front of his house. Just as we were talking about it, John walked in on his way into the city to film a cooking episode. I asked him how he came to install a little free library. I had heard about them, even saw a few here and there in my travels, but didn't really know what they were all about.

John explained that they started in Wisconsin about ten years ago by people simply wanting to share the love of reading. You can take a book, and you are encouraged to leave books that you enjoyed and want to share. There's now an official web site to register your little free library so you can see where they are. Brilliant! Imagine the growth from a handful back in 2009, to over 50,000 worldwide today. There is even one as far north as Iceland, and over a dozen in Anchorage, Alaska. John Rowe has his registered, so Pilaf is on the map. Uncle Ben said that George didn't plan to register his because it was music-specific. Perhaps George has started a brand new spin-off.

Monday, December 4, 2017, 3:08 PM

Something caught my attention when I wandered back to the front of the store. I needed a break from my usual Monday paperwork. It was too quiet and the silence was bidding me to close my eyes. Instead of caving in to the temptation, I thought that hearing the sound of my own footsteps on the wood floor would lift me out of my sleepiness. Gracie was seated at the counter, chatting softly with her neighbor, Melissa. Something looked odd. Gracie and Melissa saw me scanning past them and they turned around. I walked over to the front door and saw that the window appeared to have been vandalized. In Pilaf?

As I took a closer look, the colorful swirls appeared far too meticulous and artistically crafted. Without being able to make heads or tails out of it, I stepped out onto the front porch to examine the window. It was stunning artwork! The number "59" was in the center.

I called Officer Caputo after taking several photos. The artistry was so impressive, how could I call this vandalism? The problem was that I did not recruit anyone to do this. Even stranger was that Gracie and Melissa never heard a thing. In fact, Gracie said that she just cleaned that window no more than 30 minutes ago.

Officer Caputo arrived within minutes. He fingered the colorful swatches, then asked for water and a towel. He dipped the towel and carefully wiped one of the edges.

He simply mumbled, "Water soluble, it will all come off easily. I kind of like it. It looks festive. I'd leave it for as long as you like. But I am baffled by the number."

He paused for a moment, then turned to me and continued, "I don't think this rises to the level of vandalism. I'd be more inclined to call it mischief."

He was right. It did look beautiful and very similar in style to the sidewalk chalk art we saw before the big rain. There seemed to be a theme to it. Depictions of music, a treble clef, a G clef, quarter notes, records and CDs, all surrounded the "59" in the middle. One thing is for certain. We can't peg this one on Bonnie and Clyde.

Tuesday, December 5, 2017, 5:45 AM

If the "59" on Bailey's front window is the CLIP number, it's now too low by 2. I drove the kids on our CLIP run twice last night after dinner. Each time, they counted 61. I told them about the "59" that someone drew on Bailey's front window. They looked confused, wondering why their CLIP number mysteriously showed up on the storefront window.

They couldn't think of anyone with whom they had shared their CLIP count.

Joel and Jessie loved my open Bible and note. They said it was just like we were doing a morning devotional together, even though I wasn't there. This is a great way for me to start the day, too. While I do read in the morning at the store after the initial morning group thins out, there are days when the temptation to get busy with chores fights for my attention. Granted, it all needs to get done, but I have to remind myself that it can, and will, wait.

Tuesday, December 5, 2017, 4:01 PM

I wish I could take credit for the artistry on the window, especially given the fact that so many customers were asking me about it. It became quite the focal point today. While I suspect the number is tied somehow to the kids' CLIP number, I wasn't able to offer a clear explanation for its significance. As nifty as it looked, it was my intention to have Gracie wash it off this afternoon. Imagine my surprise when I looked out the window about a half hour ago and saw that it was as clean as a whistle. Gracie knows me very well, but how did she know I wanted the window cleaned? She didn't. After I thanked her for cleaning the artwork off the window, she said she didn't do it. Aside from a little runny watercolor on the porch, there was no evidence that the artwork had ever existed. I was going to call Officer Caputo, but what was I going to report? Someone cleaned my window? Yes, we have a delightfully quirky town, but this is getting a bit too bizarre.

It was great seeing John and Eloise enjoying lunch with the Rayburns today. Who would have thought that John Rowe would so quickly assimilate into being a Pilafian? I'm proud of everyone who lives here who made it so easy for John and his family to settle in. Pilaf isn't the kind of town that gets star-struck. Until John bought the Victorian house and moved in as a permanent resident, the closest we came to rubbing elbows with a celebrity was when we all met Stormy Windham several years ago. Come to think of it, and unbeknownst to us, John was at the apple pie contest we had two years ago, a contest for which Stormy was a judge. I'll have to see if I can arrange the two to meet sometime.

Wednesday, December 6, 2017, 7:55 AM

I love mornings like this. It was clear, cold, frosty, and calm. Orion was tipping his hat to me this morning. It's such a wonderfully easy constellation to recognize. I did catch a glimpse of Venus, but it was low on the horizon and surrounded by brighter dawn colors. George tells me that very soon, Venus will be too close to the sun to see until after New Year's Day when it wanders back into the evening sky. I don't know where I prefer Venus better, in the morning sky or evening sky.

During last evening's CLIP run, Jessie had several sneezes, one after another. There was no warning on the first one. It was so sharp to the ears that my whole body jumped. She keeps telling me there is no way to warn me when it's coming. I don't get that. I often get 15-30 seconds of feeling the sinuses tickle before I let one fly, so I can warn people around me that I'm about to sneeze.

After Jessie stopped sneezing, she asked me if we would sneeze with our new bodies in heaven. I must admit, I've never thought of that before. While some sneezes come with a brief sense of euphoria, the sneeze itself is our body trying to eject something that shouldn't be there. Because we will be raised perfect, why would we need to sneeze? Interesting speculation.

I did a word search in my Bible app before leaving the house this morning. I found two places where sneezes are mentioned. One is in 2 Kings 4:35 where Elisha brings a boy back from the dead. As he arose, he sneezed seven times. That would make sneezing a good thing in my book. The other is the sneezing of a strange creature mentioned in Job 41. I left both references out for Jessie and Joel on the kitchen table.

Mrs. Krumm was in before school started this morning. Most of her checkout items have been rather ordinary in the last year or so, but this one caught my attention. They were the ingredients for her sugar cookies, plus a jar of dill pickles. As much as I would love to know if the pickles have anything to do with this year's sugar cookie batch, we just don't ask. Secret ingredient? I shudder to think of it. Stranger still was her unexpected inquiry. She asked me if I ever carried sidewalk chalk. I told her no, but that the hardware store may carry it. I didn't think Mrs. Krumm had any interest in art. Then again, I was wrong about her sugar cookies a few years ago.

Wednesday, December 6, 2017, 2:57 PM

George came in after the lunch crowd thinned for a cup of soup. Today, it's kale soup with linguiça, a kind of Portuguese sausage that is popular wherever Portuguese is spoken. I remember trying it for the first time during a weekend getaway to Cape Cod many years ago. Last winter, Donald Buckley's mother told me that she has a wonderful recipe for the savory soup. She gladly shared it with me. It took Jimmy Giammalvo a couple of months to find a place where he could order linguiça for me. When it was introduced to our menu last winter, the lunch crowd went crazy for it. Today was the first day I brought that soup back for this winter season. Instead of being bombarded by questions asking what the meat is, this year I'm getting words of thanks for bringing back this hardy, flavorful soup.

Gracie complimented my kale soup today, a rather fine compliment considering the most popular recurring soup here at Bailey's is her creamy corn chowder. I asked her when we could work that into the rotation so that John Rowe could come and sample it. The soonest we could make room for it would be this Saturday. Gracie is up to the task, so I'll ask John if he will be available. My guess is that we are good to go since most of John's trips into the city to film episodes of his national cooking show are on weekdays.

One of the CDs that I took from George's little free CD library was playing. George immediately recognized it. You could see the delight in his face. He asked me if I had the chance to put anything into the CD box yet. I honestly don't think I have music that would interest anyone. My collection is slim. That's probably why I'm getting many positive comments on the Christmas music. Anytime there is something different playing, people notice. Perhaps I need to stop by George's box for another look to expand my selection.

George did tell me that a few people must have stopped by to add more CDs to his box. He spotted several CDs that were not there a few days ago. One was the soundtrack from the claymation television tradition, Rudolph The Red-Nosed Reindeer. George said he never did own that one and pulled it out to add to his outdoor speaker rotation for a little while. George's box was well-stocked when I pulled a few CDs to sample at Bailey's, but according to George, many more CDs are going out than coming in. I hope that trend reverses. Perhaps I should soon return the three I borrowed last weekend. When I do, I'll rely on some of the local radio stations playing all-day Christmas music to prevent Bailey's customers from hearing, ad nauseam, my limited holiday collection.

Thursday, December 7, 2017, 10:00 AM

Gabby Sauerkraut stopped in just after Mrs. Krumm left to begin her school day. The timing was rather uncanny given that Mrs. Krumm asked me if I could pass along a small box to Gabby when I saw her. Always wanting to help, and knowing how Bailey's seems to be the center of the Pilaf universe for our precious town, I took the box and placed it on the shelf over the coffee dispensers. I've been asked to do routinely innocuous things that are far more peculiar. I didn't think twice about it, that is until Gabby stopped in no more than ten minutes after Mrs. Krumm left. The rigid cardboard box was about the same size as a small loaf of bread. It wasn't very heavy but sounded like it was neatly packed with something cylindrical, like pencils or batteries. I knew they weren't batteries. The box was too light for that. It was almost too light for pencils, too. The box itself had few markings on it, no shipping labels or no company logos. I've learned not to be too nosy, but I'd be remiss if I didn't admit that I was at least a little curious. I gave the box to Gabby and she received it as if she had been expected it.

Just then, John and Eloise came in for a visit. Before I could ask Gabby any questions I would regret, I turned my attention to the Rowes and asked if they would be in town on Saturday. After verifying they'd be in town, I invited them back to sample Gracie's creamy corn chowder for lunch on Saturday. I'm sure they both get bombarded with invitations to come and taste this or sample that, but I wanted them to taste Pilaf's favorite soup. We know it's the favorite based on its sales and how busy Bailey's lunch counter is on days we have it. The word on the street spreads like wildfire when we put it on the menu.

Eloise also wanted to let me know how much they are enjoying the Sunday morning group study at church before the worship service. It was not a vague compliment. She specifically mentioned the passages I asked everyone to read before this Sunday's group study. She mentioned that she and John had started discussing them earlier in the week. So encouraging. If only everyone in the class did the same.

Thursday, December 7, 2017, 4:44 PM

The sun is still up, but so low that it's hidden behind the silhouettes of bare trees, houses, barns, and hills. The only evidence is the deep orange glow on the tips of the trees, especially the maple grove near Jasmine Creek. I could stare at that iridescent glow for hours if it stayed there. It's a color I've yet to see reproduced well in any photograph or painting. I suspect even the most alluring color here on planet Earth will seem flat compared to the colors we will see in heaven someday. In the meantime, I will relish these fleeting moments.

Once again, Pilaf is being lulled into meteorological complacency. Since Sunday's snow melt, our weather has been quiet, bright, and even somewhat humdrum. I paid closer attention to Stormy's forecast this morning, wondering if I missed something. It was as if he knew I was pondering the quiet stretch. He warned us all not to buy into the two long stretches of quiet weather since Thanksgiving. The long-term pattern should eventually change to a more active winter pattern the closer we move to Christmas and New Year's Day. I'm sure that would meet with Joel and Jessie's enthusiastic approval.

I asked Gracie to make her famous corn chowder for Saturday's soup. Her reaction was predictably nonchalant. In a very matter-of-fact fashion, she wrote the new task on a list of things she wanted to complete by the start of her weekend on Saturday. In fact, until I told her why I made my soup request, it was her intention to be gone by noon on Saturday to start an extended weekend break that included Monday. When I told her John Rowe would be coming in to taste her famous chowder, she stopped cold and her eyes opened as wide as manhole covers. She cocked her head as if to ask me if I was joking. It was all I could do to keep myself from laughing aloud at her reaction. My smile assured her though that I was not kidding. What was once the third or fourth priority on her to-do list was instantly catapulted to the top.

Gracie sighed with relief recalling that she still had some of her "secret ingredient" in her freezer. She quietly revealed her secret to me last year. I knew she was making reference to a very specific type of "supersweet" corn which is hard to find. It's called Honey 'N Pearl, a bi-color corn that was developed specifically for its ability to prevent the sugar molecules in the kernels from breaking down to starch when it is frozen. Gracie drives quite a distance to get it from a farmer in west central Ohio in early August every year. She harvests the kernels off the cob, then freezes enough to last into the winter.

During a short lull in the lunch activity, I added Friday's soup, New England clam chowder, and Saturday's soup, Gracie's creamy corn chowder, to the menu board near the counter. I recognized the corn chowder buzz from the counter. The word was out. No need to advertise. The entire town will know by tomorrow. Everything is lining up, even the weather. Stormy is calling for a cold breeze with flurries in the air. The atmosphere could not have designed a better day for soup.

Friday, December 8, 2017, 10:34 AM

George came flying in ten minutes ago, out of breath. The sidewalk chalk artist left another mark, this time right in front of George's music little free library. George stopped in on his way to the post office at 8:15 a.m. and there was nothing there. He walked by his house during the first part of his mail route and saw the artwork. He said there was a number in the middle of it, but could not remember what it was. I didn't even bother asking if George took a photo of it because his cell phone is an old flip-phone variety. It probably takes photos, but George never fiddled with it beyond making phone calls. He said it was full of color and artistry, but he could not be any more specific. He came in to ask if one of us would come and snap a photo before it mysteriously disappears like the one on my store window. The Sherlock in me figures the artist left the mark between roughly 8:15 a.m. and 10:15 a.m. My guess is whoever did it knows George's schedule, too. Where was Officer Caputo? How is it that he knows when I'm innocently meandering past George's house, but isn't anywhere nearby when our mystery artist strikes?

George needed to finish his deliveries, but he dug into his bag, all out of order, to find the mail destined for Bailey's before heading out the door half-giddy and half perplexed. There hasn't been this much intrigue in Pilaf since Bonnie and Clyde were messing with George's giant outdoor snow globe a few years ago.

The clam chowder, Pilaf's second favorite winter soup, isn't quite ready yet. I added a little more salt and a pinch of thyme and tarragon and took a taste. Perfect. Time to head to George's place with my smartphone. I might as well return the three Christmas CDs while I'm there. Perhaps I'll come back with something new.

Friday, December 8, 2017, 6:02 PM

An amazingly colorful "64" greeted me on the sidewalk square immediately in front of George's little free music library earlier today. I forgot to ask the kids what their CLIP number was last night. Chances are they are posting it somewhere in one or both of their rooms, but that surely sounds like it could be last night's count.

I'm glad I brought back the three Christmas CDs to the little free library. George was right; The selection was getting slim. I hope people start bringing some Christmas CDs to share. I did spot one in George's box that caught my attention. It was Eban Schletter's Cosmic Christmas album. I may end up regretting it, but I did pull that CD out after putting three in. I haven't sampled it yet and probably won't take a chance on it for tomorrow's soup and pie event. I'll probably pick a local radio station playing non-stop Christmas music.

Officer Caputo stopped in for some clam chowder during the lunch hour. I asked him if he knew about the sidewalk art in front of George's. He did not, but he seemed excited to check it out after finishing his lunch. I couldn't understand why this did not concern him that much, to which he simply said that as far he understood, sidewalk art was not illegal. Is it possible that Officer Caputo is doing the doodling himself? If not, could it be that the mystery artist is colluding with him? Perhaps I'm too sensitive about this whole thing since I took a direct hit on my storefront window. I hope Uncle Ben comes in tomorrow morning. He has a way of keeping things in their proper perspective and I think those lines have blurred a little for me.

Miss Marcie came in this afternoon after hearing that John Rowe was going to sample Gracie's creamy corn chowder tomorrow. She wondered if she could bake her award-winning apple pie and donate it to Bailey's, saving a large slice for John to sample. Given that, through a series of miscues, he did sample Mr. Rayburn's pie many moons ago, perhaps it's fitting that he tries Miss Marcie's pie now. That's something he's not yet had the pleasure of tasting. I accepted her kind gesture.

Mrs. Krumm came in after school let out. She meandered the aisles for a while but never put anything in her basket. Finally, her aimlessness troubled me enough to ask if I could help her locate anything. She said that she thought she had everything she needed at home, but that she wanted to be sure. Then she called me close and started whispering. I wondered why since there weren't many people in the store at the time. After hemming and hawing a little, she finally confessed her reason for stopping by. She wondered if she could make some of her Christmas sugar cookies for John Rowe's visit tomorrow. I hated to tell her that we had everything we needed already, but that she was welcome to join us all for lunch. There should be plenty for everyone.

The visits continued. Ninety-year-old Gabby Sauerkraut waltzed in and reminded me that she won second place in Pilaf's big apple pie contest two years ago. She, too, offered to bake an apple pie for John's dessert tomorrow. I didn't want to offend Gabby by telling her that Miss Marcie was bringing in hers, so I simply insisted we had everything covered. She then offered her wild mushroom soup in case we ran out of Gracie's creamy corn chowder. While I was tempted by that offer in case we had a huge crowd, I didn't want to complicate things.

The steady stream of food offers didn't stop until 4:30 p.m. Judy Brandau stopped in offering her Picalilli relish. Dave Towne wanted to bring pig's feet pie. Paula Godwin proposed making her Cajun-style boudin. The flow of offers seemed endless.

That's why I'm still here with another half hour of clean up before I can head home. The sudden brouhaha seems a little out-of-character for our town. Why all the fuss now? John and Eloise have now been Pilafians for almost two years. Maybe it's simply the excitement of Gracie's creamy corn chowder. Whatever the motive, I'm still amazed how quickly word travels in this town.

Saturday, December 9, 7:00 AM

Since Gracie had to ensure her chowder was going to be ready for today's lunch, she offered to open Bailey's. This would afford me the chance to enjoy a leisurely breakfast with the family and start the day with a short devotional. As soon as the kids wake up, we'll sip on orange juice and look at Psalm 51. It's the Scripture I've asked our Bible study group to read for this Sunday morning. It will give me a chance to refine the focus of this heartfelt prayer of David. As challenging as it may be to get the entire group to meditate on a passage before

Sunday's group study, far be it from me that I should not ask the Lord to, "create in me a pure heart, O God, and renew a steadfast spirit in me," for my own journey.

I thought I was above the flurry of inviting John over for a fun tasting today. My judgement on everyone who scrambled in line to add to today's menu was premature. My sleep was light and filled with unsettling dreams. Most of the time, I dreamed that I was in a sweaty kitchen, ladling out bowls of tasteless broth hoping that diners wouldn't notice that I didn't have any of the key ingredients for soup that would be worthy of high compliments. Finally realizing I could escape that overheated, undersupplied kitchen by simply rising from my slumber, I rose and sought the comfort of a trusted "friend," my coffee maker.

I'd like to say that the effects of waking from that kind of repeating dream was immediate. Far from it. Even after sipping my second cup of coffee during a lap visit from Sammy, his warmth prompted me to close my eyes. That's dangerous considering I still had the coffee mug in my hand. Within minutes, my body jerked as I slid toward sleep. What woke me was Sammy's back claws digging into my thighs as he bolted when my coffee sloshed up and over the mug. Sammy glanced back at me as if asking why I would do such a thing before he disappeared under the living room futon, a place where he likes to collect his thoughts.

Another surprising place I've found Sammy in recent days has been curled up near the three-foot Christmas tree. After some time had passed, he did approach and sniff the tree last year at the end of the Christmas season, but he never slept anywhere near it. After witnessing its stability for two consecutive seasons, my guess is that Sammy felt comfortable enough to cozy up to the unassuming tree with the soft glow. I don't have a photo yet, but I'm hoping to preserve that peaceful scene this year.

The pre-dawn sky look dark and gray. No snow. No flurries. It's 22°F. What a great day for soup.

Saturday, December 9, 9:55 PM

It was one of those days that seemed to fly by so fast that you wondered how time managed to accelerate out of control. Why is it that boring or challenging days never seem to end, while the ones filled with fun and joy zip by? I'm glad we have all of eternity to enjoy the unspeakable joy in heaven. In the meantime, I'll relish the praiseworthy days that we experience on this side of eternity.

My arrival at Bailey's was memorable. I actually smelled Gracie's creamy corn chowder long before I reached the front door. Imagine how much more fragrant our best-selling soup was once I stepped inside! Even though I just enjoyed a huge waffle and sausage breakfast at home with the family, I was tempted to ladle a sample. I knew better. Gracie would have chased me around the stove with whatever object was nearby to protect her soup. As tempted as I was, I knew it needed another hour before all of the flavors were released. I had to be satisfied with the mouth-watering aroma.

Uncle Ben was already there. Normally, he would have had at least one cherry Danish and several cups of coffee by now, but he did not want to spoil his appetite. He was sipping a glass of orange juice, waiting for the first bowl of soup to come out of the kitchen. Since we needed to pass some time, I sat down with him and asked what he would do about the mysterious chalk and window artist running loose. I knew he could add the perspective that I needed. First, there was no clean-up needed. Either the rain did the work, or in my case, the window was washed and sparkling clean a few days later. Second, it was starting to bring the town together. Perhaps whoever is creating this artwork is trying to focus the town on something fun. At first, I didn't understand what Uncle Ben meant. He went on to explain that he thought there may be clues in the artwork that pointed to where the next appearance would be. The artwork on my window, for instance, was music-themed. Where was the most recent? It was in front of George's music little free library. He suggested we put all of our heads together to see if we could figure out where the next one would be based on the artwork that surrounded the number. I was no longer bothered by the peculiar artwork. Since I snapped photos of the most recent work, I would take a closer look with the family to see if we could predict where the next one would occur.

Pilaf was starting to arrive. Everyone who came through the door had an expression of delight as they took in the aroma of Gracie's chowder. It was going to be an unusually busy weekend lunch hour. The counter and tables filled up quickly, all except for two seats with a reserved placard on them. Uncle Ben and George both arrived so early, that they claimed a seat on either side of where the Rowes would be seated. By the time Jennifer, Joel, and Jessie arrived, all the tables were taken. Uncle Ben and George must have seen the disappointment on the kid's faces. Now standing by their seats, they simultaneously waved Joel and Jessie over and hoisted them onto the counter seats with symphonic precision. The more I think about it, the more I believe this was their plan all along.

John and Eloise arrived at exactly noon. The clouds shook loose storybook snow flurries like confetti as they were seen walking the short distance from their home to Bailey's. Everyone applauded when the door opened.

"Wow! You might think someone important just walked in," John pronounced with humility.

I showed John and Eloise to their seats and waited for a lull in the chatter before asking for everyone's attention. I called Gracie to stand beside me, and, Jennifer turned down the Christmas music on cue. After thanking everyone for coming, I let Gracie announce the surprise. Today's soup luncheon was on-the-house with Bailey's compliments. The reaction was priceless!

Gracie then excused herself to serve the first two bowls to John and Eloise, who up to now had never tasted Gracie's creamy corn chowder. The look of genuine amazement in their eyes as they tasted Pilaf's favorite winter soup is something I'll enjoy replaying in my mind for many seasons to come. Their expressions were virtually identical when they tasted Miss Marcie's apple pie.

Because there was only standing room, as people finished their soup, they offered up their tables and counter seats to others in a way that much of the world wouldn't understand. By 1:30 p.m., everyone had been served. There was even enough corn chowder left to send home two quart containers with John and Eloise, but all the apple pie was gone.

George, Uncle Ben, Jennifer, Joel, and Jessie all stayed to help clean up after the crowd was gone. I placed the very strange Christmas CD by Eban Schletter back into George's hands to put it back into his CD box. He laughed and didn't have to ask if I liked it. George brought a few Christmas CDs from his own personal collection to play while we cleaned up.

Having had a restless night's sleep, I was fading just as quickly as the daylight through the clouds. It was still snowing ever so lightly, but not really accumulating. I suggested having a pizza night out in Borger. No one resisted.

On the drive home, I asked the kids if it was okay if we crafted our route home to get their CLIP number. Their eyes were heavy, but I could see them smile in approval.

Everyone is already fast asleep. It took everything I had to write today's journal entry, but I did not want to fall asleep before accurately painting the day's joy. Time has a way of obscuring the details that make events special, but time did not steal away today before I set it in stone. A deep sleep awaits. I hope it's as sweet as Gracie's creamy corn chowder.

Sunday, December 10, 2017, 9:22 AM

Thank goodness Jennifer had the foresight to cook up a batch of Dutch Baby pancakes last night. We all ignored the bright sunshine wake up call. No one set an alarm either. The first one up was Jennifer, but it was 7:30 a.m. so she let us sleep as late as possible. She stirred the kids first, then me. By 8:30 a.m., we were all wobbling down the stairs and into an aromatic kitchen.

Looks like a great day ahead. The weather is still pretty quiet. Pilaf's Christmas decorations need a little snowfall. Stormy keeps talking about a change in the weather pattern soon. I think I'll email him tomorrow.

I hope our morning Bible study class is prepared this week. I'm anxious to dig in with others who are eagerly anticipating movement of the Holy Spirit.

Sunday, December 10, 2017, 5:00 PM

Jennifer has several candles lit in the kitchen and one in the den. It's something we can do to combat the earliest sunset of the year, now just before 5 o'clock. Of course, the Christmas lights have the same effect. I think about people in Australia or Chile who are in their meteorological summer. For them, Christmas comes with long days, short nights, swimwear, short-sleeved shirts, and lemonade. For natives of those countries in the southern hemisphere, that's perfectly normal. I must admit, at the very least, that would be extremely odd for us. Getting the CLIP number every night would be a very late-night chore.

Drake & Vicki piled into our van after church today. They heard our kids talking about decorating Bailey's and wanted to join the festivities. It's fun seeing the cousins play together. I can't ever imagine a time when our kids and Jim and Barb's kids will ever drift far from each other.

I dropped Jennifer off at the house on our way to the store so she could have some quiet time while the rest of us tackled the decorating. I like every day at Bailey's, but going there when the store is closed is very likely my favorite time. There are no chores, no crowds, and no deadlines. Granted, I like the "crowds" during the week. Without them, I couldn't pay the bills. But having the whole store as a playground of sorts on a Sunday afternoon reminds me of why we moved from the city.

Joel and Jessie pulled out paper and pens to try to plan out how they envisioned decorating for Christmas this year. Drake and Vicki loved being part of the planning phase. As soon as that was done though, I noticed they weren't exactly eager to start tackling the task itself. It didn't take long for me to figure out why, and I didn't even need to inquire. After staring out the window for a few minutes, they wandered over to me and asked if they could take a short walk down the Jasmine Creek footpath. They mentioned that it would feel strange decorating without having the ambience of snow falling or even seeing snow on the ground. I get that. Snow does have a way of adding that "je ne sais quoi" to this time of year.

As the kids were suiting up for an early winter's walk to Jasmine Creek together, I noticed John Rowe walking toward the store. As the kids walked out, John walked up the stairs, popped his head in the door and asked if it was okay to come in. He knew Bailey's was closed, but took a chance that I might be hanging out here. I asked him how he knew. He said that the same passion he has for food makes a restful Sunday in the kitchen exceedingly pleasurable. He sees the passion I have for the store and the people who frequent Bailey's and thought I might be here for a little while. Touché.

He wanted to thank me again for setting up the soup tasting in a way that was so much fun for him and Eloise. He also wanted to tell me that he would love to highlight Gracie's corn chowder and Miss Marcie's famous apple pie recipes in one of his winter cooking programs. Wow! I'm certain they'd be honored. Pilaf, Ohio might become much more than just a little dot on a map.

We also talked about this morning's Bible study class. I was pleased that about half of the group read Psalm 51. I was cautiously optimistic that more people would arrive having meditated on it. John and Eloise's contribution this morning was deep and meaningful. Even Harry Buser, who two years ago had little interest in our study group, had some amazing observations to share. John must have sensed my disappointment with others who don't come prepared. I'm happy they are all there and hopefully walking away with tools to navigate life, but how deep can the wisdom sink in so that it is recalled with ease?

I told John that I was tempted to bring doughnuts in and give them out only to those who could either answer quiz questions or contribute to the discussion. Bribe them with doughnuts? I can't believe I actually entertained that idea. We were both chuckling when suddenly, John stopped and looked up. There was a curious gleam in his eyes. After a few seconds, he froze with a neutral expression. Finally, a little smile. He said he had an idea, but needed some time to think it through before he shared it. Fair enough.

The kids busted in the front door with so much excitement, it sounded like more than a dozen kids storming in. They had something to show me. Joel emptied his coat pocket onto one of the tables. John and I walked over for a closer look. There were two used sticks of sidewalk chalk and a muddy handkerchief. One chalk stick was bright green, the other red. They said they found them at the base of one of the giant maple trees. They asked if they could keep their find. I'm glad they were making reference to the chalk and not the handkerchief. They asked if they could try drawing something in the parking lot. I didn't see any harm in it.

Monday, December 11, 2017, 7:21 AM

I looked for Venus on my way to Bailey's this morning, but could not find it. Once again, skies are delightfully clear. There is not a whisper of wind and it's not all that cold. Orion is now dipping low in the western sky, making most of its presence a few hours after the sun sets. Joel and Jessie are right. As festive as the Christmas lights look, they all seem to be pleading for a little snowfall.

I emailed Stormy Windham this morning. I invited him over to Bailey's for lunch to meet John Rowe. I also told him about George's latest Christmas addition, his music little free library. At last check, the CD collection was dwindling quickly, so I told him the sooner the better before all the CDs disappeared.

Stormy was on the radio ten minutes ago. He still insists on a pattern change that will give our Christmas lights the aura that they are calling for by the end of the week.

The kids left the green and red sidewalk chalk on one of the tables yesterday. It was my intention to stash them somewhere else before customers started coming in, but my Monday routine blanked it out. Mrs. Krumm came in before the school day began and spotted them on the table. She brought them to the counter and wondered if she could take them. I told her about how the kids found them near the Jasmine Creek footpath beneath a maple tree. Figuring they were finished with the chalk, I told her she could have them. Why would Mrs. Krumm want sidewalk chalk? There is no way she is the mystery artist we are looking for. As much as I wanted to probe, I stopped myself. We simply don't ask.

Monday, December 11, 2017, 1:49 PM

We went from bright sunshine to thick clouds in the matter of an hour at midday. No rain. No snow. Still not much wind spare a puff or two, but it looks as dark as late afternoon.

Uncle Ben stopped by for a mid-morning chat and a cup of minestrone soup. It was ready before the lunchtime rush. He said he initially came in for a cup of coffee, but smelled the soup and knew it was ready. Good nose. That did not surprise me nearly as much as when he asked if I would give John Rowe a container of his gortons spread to try. Uncle Ben too? It seems as though having a well-known chef in our midst has brought out the chefs in us all. I won't be hard on him, though. While I have not personally whipped anything up for John, I did organize the soup tasting to highlight Gracie's corn chowder here at Bailey's.

While Mrs. Krumm took the leftover sidewalk chalk this morning, she apparently had no interest in the muddy handkerchief that was still on the windowsill near the front door. Like the chalk, I kept meaning to pick it up and throw it away. Uncle Ben spotted it and asked me how his handkerchief got so muddy. His handkerchief? I told him where the kids found it. He insisted he had one missing from his supply. Sure enough, when he wiped away enough of the dirt and mud from one of the corners, you could see his monogram. I'm not convinced that washing it would restore it, but he did take it anyway. We both looked at each other wondering how it ended up deep in the woods by the creek. Could he tell I was wondering if Uncle Ben is the stealth artist? After all, the sidewalk chalk and his handkerchief were found in the same place.

Tuesday, December 12, 2017, 10:00 AM

This morning's soft, low light filtered through the heavy cloud deck and light rain brought out the best of the Christmas lights in the store today. I did not realize how bright sunshine can quietly steal the warm glow of this Christmas cheer. Except a few quick visits from George, Officer Caputo, and a couple of the teachers from the school, it was fairly quiet. Bailey's had that cozy Christmas feeling again.

George delivered a Christmas card from the Linakers in Fleetwood, England today. It came with a photo of their town square, cozy with lights. Sunset comes even earlier in Fleetwood. Add the almost constant drizzly skies of England and the Christmas lights have a perpetual cozy gleam. I'll remind Jennifer to make certain the Linakers are on our Christmas newsletter mailing list.

Stormy called me this morning after his last live radio segment on WPLF about a half-hour ago. He asked if both John and George would be in town on Thursday. His thought was to make the drive down here before the weather closes in on Friday. He has a surprise for George but asked me to keep that info close to my vest. It helps that I have no idea what that surprise is. Stormy offered no other details. I'm certain that both will be delighted with his visit.

I'll check on their schedules but told Stormy to plan on a late lunch at Bailey's.

Tuesday, December 12, 2017, 4:58 PM

The morning round of light rain tapered off to drizzle by lunchtime. Everything is wet. There is little chance we will see any new sidewalk art show up on a day like today. With a snowier pattern setting in on Friday, perhaps the sidewalk chalk artist will take a break.

Uncle Ben wandered in for lunch today, but hung out well past the peak of the lunch crowd. He was hoping I had enough time to look over the photos of the most recent sidewalk art by George's music little free library. Tuesday is typically a good day for extra free time. Uncle Ben remembered that. He also thought, as I did, that no new artwork would pop up today with everything being so wet. Before sitting down with him, I thought about my brief suspicion that Uncle Ben was the artist we were looking for. For a number of reasons though, that's

FOOD FOR THE SOUL

virtually impossible, not the least of which is his increasing immobility. Uncle Ben's back could never stand the time it would take to draw such intricate things. Come to think of it, I don't think I've ever seen him draw so much as a stick figure. How his handkerchief, along with two pieces of sidewalk chalk, ended up near the Jasmine Creek footpath is also beyond me. Uncle Ben prefers staying on smooth, paved surfaces. I hope he doesn't think I even entertained the idea that he was a possible suspect. I'd be embarrassed to admit it.

I already transferred the photos from my smartphone to my digital tablet. They were much easier to examine together. The clues were small, but there seemed to be a theme. All around the number 64 were various objects that appeared to be in motion in a circle around the number. The only item that seemed identifiable was what we both surmised was a police car. It was clear that it was chasing something. What could that mean? We both started tossing out ideas, but none of them seemed reasonable.

Joel and Jessie stopped in after school with a couple of their friends. When they galloped their way through the front door, my Bible was open on the counter as I was meditating on a verse in Ephesians Chapter 2, a verse that says God actually seated us with Christ in the heavenly realm. Too many times it doesn't "feel" like it, but we have to move past that and realize that God means what He says and says what He means. This is the passage I'll be looking at in the Sunday morning Bible class. Joel and Jessie came over and asked me what passage I was looking at. I read the passage to them, and they seemed to grab hold of it faster and with greater enthusiasm than I'd expect from most adults.

I told them about the snow coming at the end of the week. They beamed. I asked them if they would like to come back with their friends to decorate this weekend. Their beams doubled in brightness. I'll take that as a yes.

Wednesday, December 13, 2017, 9:48 AM

The weather must have cleared out overnight since the waning crescent moon greeted me, looking like a bull's horn, on my way to the store this morning. According to George, Venus is still rising before the sun, but only by 30 minutes. Without a telescope that is properly positioned, few human eyes have ever seen it when it was so close to the sun.

Mr. Rayburn stopped in before his school day started. He asked if any of us had seen what looked like window art on the police station's front window. Uncle Ben arrived minutes after Mr. Rayburn and asked the same thing. Both saw the number "86" in the middle of the window. The word spread fast. As the sun rose higher, and as there was more light to snap photos, customers grabbed their coffee and morning pastries to drive to the police station. I asked Uncle Ben if he was interested in heading over there with me once the bulk of the morning chores were finished. I'm glad he agreed. I think he's onto something regarding pictorial clues that point to the location of the next piece of artwork. The last one had what looked like a police car chasing objects around the number.

We haven't seen Officer Caputo yet today. My guess is that he is not a happy camper right now. It's one thing to investigate erasable window and sidewalk art at various locations, but when it's created on the police station's window, this so-called "mischief" may have occurred in the wrong place. Officer Caputo has always been able to get to the bottom of oddities here in Pilaf. If my guess is right, he has already placed this mystery on the fast-track to being solved.

A wintry breeze is blowing today. Despite the bright sun, it's a crisp wind. Other winds have been colder than this one, but there is something about its smell that is announcing winter is about ready to roost in Pilaf.

Wednesday, December 13, 2017, 3:33 PM

I glanced up at the clock and saw 3:33 p.m. Only then did I remember my brief stirring early this morning when I saw my clock at 3:33 a.m. I stirred from an odd dream and I was glad to have had the chance to shake it off, but now I cannot remember what that odd dream was about. It's just as well since I do remember feeling relieved that it was only a dream.

Officer Caputo waltzed in for lunch today when I was in the kitchen. It was relatively busy. The cacophony of chatter from the counter suddenly stopped. It reminded me of how the cackling of chickens in a chicken coop stops if anyone makes an unusual sound, something brother Jim and I did for kicks at our uncle's egg farm when we were young. When I walked out to see why the chatter suddenly dropped, I saw several people standing around Officer Caputo while he answered questions about the new artwork. It took a few minutes, but he gradually made his way to an open counter seat to order lunch. I told Gracie that his lunch was on the house today, something I like to do to honor those who serve to keep us safe.

I waited until he was almost finished with his lunch to ask about the new artwork. Knowing he had been bombarded by curious townsfolk earlier, I was a bit more casual in bringing up the topic. Much to my surprise, Officer Caputo was far less irritated about the whole affair. He simply shrugged it off as yet more mischief while offering a smile that communicated he could not do much about it. He did say that he would be cleaning it off at the end of his shift later today, and that it was not a big deal and easy to remove. His reaction gave me a deeper respect for his steady-state. It was the very same reaction when he examined the artwork on my front window at Bailey's. There was no difference when the target's canvas was the police station's front window. His easy-going style reminds me of Sheriff Andy Taylor's character on The Andy Griffith Show. The sheriff always got his man, but it was always with a steady-state smile.

Uncle Ben and I did wander over to the police station. It was a nice day and I could have walked, but I did not want to tax Uncle Ben's knees. They've been bothering him recently, so I insisted that I drive us there. I snapped photos of the artwork, but it was hardly necessary. It was obvious that the number "86" was pressed neatly inside an outline of the United Kingdom. A locator star was placed just a little above the "8" along the west coast. Was the locator star random or was it there for a reason? Uncle Ben and I will look on a map to see if there are any clues waiting for discovery.

Thursday, December 14, 2017, 7:40 AM

The Pilaf Register is always thicker in December. It's not so much the added holiday ads and flyers that make it thick, but rather the volume of news. Ever since I could remember, December has never been a boring month around Pilaf. Today's edition is a good example. Just as I sat at the counter with a cup of coffee and the paper, John Rowe came in holding up the same paper. There were four photos, side-by-side, across the top with a big, bold headline: MYSTERY ARTIST STRIKES AGAIN. Each photo showed the sidewalk or window art that appeared around town. Of course, one of those photos was Bailey's front window. Free advertising on the front page! Such a deal. While a fair share of people in Pilaf had at least heard about it, this morning's paper will make certain everyone is in the know.

John asked me if I had seen it yet. A few minutes ago, I would have told him no. Only then did I have enough time to sit for a moment and read the morning paper. This art caper is grabbing so much of our attention that I'm concerned many people may have missed Stormy's forecast. Does anyone know that a snowy assault will be greeting us tomorrow? I usually see an uptick of traffic in the store by now. Aside from a few customers, some just dropping by for a casual visit, Bailey's has been oddly quiet this morning. We are well stocked and ready for any last-minute rush.

The quieter pace has actually worked to our advantage since we are ready for Stormy's visit later today. His final live radio feed after WPLF at 9:10 a.m. is WCCZ-FM, a station in Coshocton, at 9:20 a.m. Adding time to wrap up his work day, Stormy should be arriving a little before 1 o'clock. I'm glad he's coming for a visit. It has been almost two years since he surprised us all by being one of the apple pie judges on New Year's Eve, 2015. I sure would love to see him spend a weekend here. He could stay with us and come and go as he pleases. While it's not my motive, it would be fun to lure Stormy so that he made Pilaf his home base. Having two big media names in Pilaf would be something special.

We had a stunning sunrise today. The high clouds were just coming in, the first signature of an approaching storm. The sky turned the brightest, most iridescent pink I've seen in a very long time. This kind of dazzling brilliance usually doesn't last all but a handful of minutes. Today's show lasted almost ten minutes, putting a surreal pink glow inside Bailey's.

Thursday, December 14, 2017, 6:38 PM

I should have known how quickly word spreads in this town, especially when I'm the source of the news. Bailey's went from quiet to suddenly noisy just before the lunch rush hit. It had little to do with the impending snowfall, rather the prognosticator of the precipitation himself. Almost everyone who came in asked when Stormy was going to arrive, and this was after John and Eloise were already seated at one of the larger tables. We were all waiting for the Rayburns and Stormy. Mr. Rayburn arranged for one of the other teachers to pinch hit for Miss Marcie's class for a short while so that they could all enjoy each other's company and surely reminisce about the apple pie baking contest. The Pilaf Register even sent over a photographer to snap a photo for tomorrow morning's paper. Yet more great (and free) press. Lucky me!

Both Stormy and the Rayburns came up the porch steps at the same time. They both arrived earlier than expected. It was 12:40 p.m. The next hour had a festive feel, almost as electric as the apple pie baking contest. While everyone took photos, they all traded stories and laughter while enjoying potato-leek soup and turkey croissant sandwiches.

With the Rayburns needing to return to school and the Rowes obliged to drive to Lodi for a speaking engagement, the crowd quickly thinned. George arrived as everyone was heading out the door. I asked him to stop by because Stormy said he had something for him. Sure enough, Stormy had a large box that he never opened or moved until George arrived. The handful of customers that remained all leaned in when George was given the box to open. George's expression lit up in amazement when he saw more than a hundred Christmas CDs for his little free library. George said there were only three CDs that remained. This re-supply was arriving at the perfect time. I encouraged George to put a bigger sign outside his music box that invited people to come and share some of their Christmas CDs.

Stormy wanted to see the little free library, as he had never seen one. Not only did he see George's, but also John and Eloise's little free library for books. That was three hours ago. Stormy is surely home by now preparing for what is likely to be his busiest day of this season thus far. Skies became overcast and much gloomier before sunset. The snow hasn't started falling yet, but you can actually smell it coming. It's something I would have a difficult time trying to describe verbally.

I hope it's snowing by the time I drive the kids on their CLIP run. I love seeing the excitement on their faces.

Friday, December 15, 2017, 7:09 AM

Our CLIP run was as late as I could make it without disrupting the kid's bedtime routine. I kept the deck flood light on hoping to see the first flakes, but the clouds were uncooperative when we piled into the car. I don't know who was more disappointed, me or the kids. That disappointment didn't last long. By the time we reached Bailey's, a very light, fine snow had started to float in my headlights. The mood shifted from ordinary to magical as we slowly made our way back to the house, listening to a Glen Campbell Christmas CD. The world may have lost him, but knowing his faith testimony and knowing he is offering his voice in heaven allows me to play his music with a sense of Christmas joy.

While I was hoping the snow would start for our CLIP drive, there is a downside that I frequently forget (or choose to ignore). The youthful adrenalin was now flowing through Joel and Jessie. Their eyelids were not heavy at all. Their heads did not want to make contact with their pillows. Animated chatter included the speculation of a snow day. Both Jennifer and I had to simply smile at the extra effort needed to settle them down and encourage them to fall asleep. I'm certain they were jumping out of their skin when they learned that all schools in the area had canceled classes for today, our first snow day of the year.

The overnight snow was light, but persistent. The very fine snow and very cold air made travel quite slippery this morning. As he thought, Stormy will have a longer Friday than normal. He expects the snow to persist all day and into tonight before ending. I'm glad he was able to visit yesterday.

The pop from the sound of the plows hitting potholes and bumps in the road sounded familiar. It almost sounded like a cross between the two kinds of pops that Jennifer and I heard on the tennis court many months ago. When we were on the court alone, our main focus was simply volleying the ball as long as we could. Our main exercise came from chasing the sometimes wild returns to each other. We thought we were doing well until two young high school girls occupied the court beside us. The sound of their volleys were starkly different from ours. With seemingly very little effort, the sound of the tennis ball hitting their rackets sounded like a hard, commanding pop. The sound coming from our tennis rackets sounded more like a loose string on a poorly made guitar being plucked. The sound of our volley gave away our amateur attempt at tennis. While embarrassment would have been easy, we gave it no thought since our goal was to simply break a sweat, something we did while giving chase to comical, uncontrolled volleys.

Friday, December 15, 2017, 2:57 PM

It's still snowing, but only very lightly now. It's the kind of snow that doesn't seem to accumulate. The snowplows must be back in the local road department garages. I haven't seen one since around 1 o'clock.

Jennifer stopped by with Joel and Jessie a few hours ago. Jennifer needed to run a few errands and wondered if the kids could stay here. Since there was snow on the ground, and in the air, they could finally entertain the thought of planning out their contribution for Bailey's Christmas decorations. They've been busy running around the store with their pads and pens, pointing everywhere.

Just a little after 2 o'clock, Officer Caputo came up the porch stairs at the same time as John Rowe. I retreated to the back office for an inventory form and to look up a phone number I needed. It had to be at least three minutes before I returned to the counter, fully expecting to see Officer Caputo and John seated together, but they weren't there. They were still standing in the same position on the porch, looking serious as they talked. John made a motion as if he was getting cold. That's when they finally came through the front door. I made light of their long chat outside and asked if John needed bail. Officer Caputo said yes, and that a bowl of my clam chowder would work. John laughed and said since it was his bail, he might as well have a taste of it as well.

I grabbed a little chowder for myself and sat opposite them. John suggested that I drive by their place tonight. His Christmas decorations are finally up. Last year, his decorations were very modest, but tastefully done. John and Eloise did not have the opportunity to break out all of their decorations. One year ago, most of them were still in moving boxes. Not so this year! Joel heard John's invitation and popped out from the second floor balcony. He asked John if everything would be on tonight. When he replied that they would, both Joel and Jessie squealed with delight. Their CLIP number would increase by at least one.

Wondering if I would get any questions from Officer Caputo or John Rowe, I asked the kids what last night's "CLIP number" was. They immediately replied in unison, "93." I waited for curiosity to drive either Officer Caputo or John to ask me what the CLIP number was. Nothing. They just kept slurping their soup.

Saturday, December 16, 2017, 8:01 AM

Gracie opened up the store today so I could enjoy breakfast at home and do a little work on Sunday's Bible study at church. No more snow was expected overnight, so there would be no outdoor cleanup needed. In fact, skies are as brilliant and clear as a flawless blue diamond.

I still don't know what John Rowe has in mind in helping to get more people to prepare for our group Bible study. Something tells me I'll find out this Sunday.

In the meantime, the topic at breakfast this morning was what we saw on our CLIP run last night. John and Eloise's decorations elevated the CLIP number to 94. That, however, is not the most noteworthy item. It was the way they decorated the outside of their home. When their home came into view, our jaws dropped. Jennifer came with us last night and she wondered why Joel, Jessie, and I were staring in disbelief. To Jennifer, it was a wonderful display of Christmas cheer. Jennifer never saw what this house looked like two Christmases ago. It was decorated exactly as we remember it from our CLIP runs that year, the house that pushed the CLIP number to one hundred for two nights. It was also the same house that Adrienne Camp showed me close up after Christmas Day. It was abandoned.

The insides were being gutted and renovated. Furthermore, the power was turned off for some electrical work. If it was a figment of our imagination, why did all three of us see the same thing? We never did figure that one out. It's as if we caught a glimpse into the future that night.

Saturday, December 16, 2017, 5:17 PM

The first few appearances of the mystery artwork had a limited audience. By the time the stealth artist found a canvas on the front window of the police station, many more people were talking about it. Between the photos on the front page of the Pilaf Register two days ago and all the radio chatter about the newest masterpiece on WPLF this morning, there isn't a soul who lives in Pilaf who isn't talking about it. The latest colorful spread was on the front window of Giammalvo's Market this morning.

Uncle Ben was waiting for me when I walked through Bailey's front door. I knew something was up. The clamor of customer chatter didn't sound as relaxed as it normally does on a Saturday morning. As I walked toward Uncle Ben, who kept his gaze on me, I gleaned bits and pieces of conversations as I walked toward the counter.

"Could the artist be so-and-so?"

"Where do you think the next one will show up?"

"I think the numbers mean this-or-that."

No one was talking about the weather, the coffee, politics, or anything else.

I asked Uncle Ben if he had his Danish.

"Long gone," he replied, "so let's go."

Gracie had everything under control, so Uncle Ben and I drove to Jimmy Giammalvo's store. When we arrived , there were more than a dozen people gawking at the newest window art. Every sidewalk was covered with snow and ice from Friday's snowfall so sidewalk chalk art would have been near impossible to create.

The number in the middle was "94." That was last night's CLIP number! Jennifer and I were the only two people with Joel and Jessie last night when we made our CLIP run. As easy as it would have been to entertain the thought of an inside job, I quickly dismissed any notion that Jennifer had anything to do with this. Could it be coincidence? I don't think so. But how? Why Giammalvo's Market?

Since Uncle Ben seems to have become wise to clues that point to the next location, I dared him to make sense of this one based on a map of the United Kingdom. Jimmy is 100% Italian. Uncle Ben reminded me that two years ago, Jimmy and Alice's good friends, Craig and Anne Linaker were in Pilaf not once, but twice during the Christmas season. Craig and Anne live in Fleetwood, a coastal town roughly where the star was on the drawn map. The only connection that Fleetwood, UK, has in Pilaf is Jimmy and Alice Giammalvo. Brilliant. I'm tempted to start calling him Uncle Sherlock. I would have never made the connection.

I took photos with my smartphone. I'll be paying far more attention to what he sees in this design.

Sunday, December 17, 2017, 6:55 AM

We woke to more light snow this morning. Everything looks a little brighter with fresh snow cover, even before dawn breaks. I accidentally left the outdoor Christmas lights on last night, so their reflected glow softly filled nearly every room. After briefly turning on the back deck light, I saw about an inch or two of fresh powder. It had a very cold look to it. That was verified when I saw 16°F on the thermometer outside the kitchen window. Stormy sure nailed this pattern shift. He was on the money.

Sammy is curled under our miniature Christmas tree in the living room. I saw him stretch and yawn when I walked past him, but he showed no interest in following me to the kitchen. I'm sure that will change if he smells food. It's nice to see him getting over the intimidation and aversion to Christmas trees. Granted, this one is not so intimidating.

I told Jennifer and the kids about the window art at Giammalvo's Market last night at dinner. Joel and Jessie's eyes grew as big as Jennifer's Mount Mansfield apple pie in a state of bewilderment that went beyond words. They asked me how anyone would know what their CLIP number could be. I was hoping they could offer even the smallest clue. When that didn't happen, I had to admit that I had no answers.

Sunday, December 17, 2017, 9:37 PM

Pilaf looks so festive decorated with snow. The clouds must have been pretty thick today. During our drive to church, we easily saw homes whose occupants kept their outdoor Christmas lights on. Perhaps part of this was due to not enough light to trigger the automatic daylight sensors. Part of me wants to believe it's deliberate, adding that beautiful Christmas ambience. I pre-loaded Vince Guaraldi's Charlie Brown Christmas CD in the car last night so it would be our music backdrop. It doesn't get any better.

After getting the kids settled in the youth ministry area, Jennifer and I walked into our adult study room. As we approached the door, we could see that something was different. Once inside, the warmth of the Christmas lights that lit up the room made us both smile. Something else struck me. The decorations looked identical to what I saw in the classroom two years ago. Back then, no one knew (or seemed to care) who had done the decorating. I dared to ask again. This time, John and Eloise Rowe stepped toward us and asked us if we liked it. Of course! It was wonderful!

John mentioned that this spring, they found several large boxes in the attic. They were loaded with all kinds of Christmas decorations. He and

Eloise contacted the former owner, but discovered that the decorations were not theirs. After testing the lights and seeing that everything was in fine, working order, they decided to decorate their house with the lights this Christmas. After they finished, they used the remainder of them to decorate the adult classroom at church. They convinced the church caretaker, Bob LaMoreaux, to let them in early this morning, well before anyone else arrived. Like quantum physics, sometimes you simply have to accept what you're seeing, and enjoy it as Christmas magic. Like every peculiar encounter with Mrs. Krumm, we just don't ask.

Before we started our study, John asked if he could speak to everyone. He came up front and made a special announcement. He was going to host a very special formal dinner in the fellowship hall on Christmas Eve night. He was bringing in several guest chefs for a night of heavy hor d'oeuvres and appetizers as the first seating of a two-part dinner spaced exactly one week apart, all at no-charge. It was their gift to Pilaf. There would be one hundred seats available and he was giving the Bible study class the first chance to sign up. Any remaining seats would be opened, first-come, first-served, to the rest of the church members. John and Eloise's announcement received a grateful response. I caught a few people closing their eyes and taking a deep breath in through their noses as if they could smell the banquet.

By the time class was over, John had 55 people signed up. After making the same announcement during the service, the remaining 45 seats were snapped up after the congregation was dismissed.

Jim and Barb invited us over for dinner tonight. It has been a while since we've had the chance to bring the two families together for an evening of food and fun. When we arrived, we all smiled when we saw the miniature pine tree at the driveway entrance. While not even close to being mature, the mini-tree is not-so-mini anymore. It's almost two feet taller compared to when Drake insisted on putting blue LED lights on it three years ago. This time, it was lit with sparkling blue icicle lights. It looked grand! Later, when everyone was settled, Jim motioned me over. We went outside and walked up to the tree. He showed me how he could control it from his smartphone. Drake was out of sight, so he changed it to sparkling white icicle lights. Too funny.

Barb asked me if I knew what John Rowe's upcoming spread on Christmas Eve was all about. I had to honestly say that I did not know. John did say he had an idea that would encourage more people to read the Bible daily, but I'm not convinced this is a part of that plan. I've considered food bribery myself, but something inside me thinks a plan like that could easily backfire.

After a wonderful meal followed by a round of Scrabble, Jennifer and I rounded up the kids to head home and prepare for the week ahead. It will be a short week for Joel and Jessie but a long one for me. On the way out the driveway, I had to laugh. The icicle lights were blue again. Something tells me this battle will go on for years.

Monday, December 18, 2017, 7:49 AM

It's another cold morning. Stormy is forecasting several light, snowy systems through the end of the week. Looks like our snow is on the ground to stay through much, if not all, of the holiday period. There was a collective sigh when the snow arrived last week. Last year, December was largely snowless. There wasn't even a hint of old snow on the ground on Christmas Day. In fact, all of last winter was mild and quiet.

Uncle Ben was the first to arrive this morning just after 6 o'clock. I was expecting him. The coffee was on and Maureen Whittles from Giammalvo's Market had already dropped off my pastry order. The cherry Danishes were still warm from the oven.

I brought my extra large digital tablet so we could closely examine the newest window art for clues that may lead to the next design. Uncle Ben got a head start while I reheated the Danish and poured the coffee. As I returned to the table, Uncle Ben was shaking his head. He was having trouble making any sense of the artwork around the giant "94."

After looking at everything together in the same frame, I suggested breaking it down into quadrants. Uncle Ben had no objections. He suggested we start at the top, and scan clockwise. I kept a yellow legal pad handy to jot some notes. The first image looked like either a box or a book. Whatever it was had a number "2" on it. The image at the 4 o'clock position was easy. Both of us saw a clock which appeared to be showing 7:30. In the 7 o'clock position was something that resembled a skinny roll tied by a blue ribbon in the middle. In the 9 o'clock position, another easy image. It was clearly an apple. Finally, in the 11 o'clock position, another somewhat rectangular shape. It was brown. At first we thought it was a solid color, but a second photo that was more in focus showed a very thin, black mark that looked like the number "222" at the very top.

None of the images made sense to us. They didn't seem to have anything in common. We may need some serious help with this one.

Monday, December 18, 2017, 4:07 PM

It was fun seeing Joel and Jessie walk into Bailey's after school let out today. Their rosy cheeks gave away the Christmas chill they encountered on their short walk from the school. They were thrilled with how festive everything looked in the store. I reminded them they had something to do with that, to which they both smiled broadly. Much to their credit, they settled at a quiet table and broke out their homework. They said they did not have much to do, but wanted to get it all finished before dinner tonight. Tomorrow should be an easy school day since Wednesday's classes will be dismissed at noon for Christmas break. Jennifer picked them up about a half-hour ago on her way home from the Ohio Station Outlets in Lodi for a little Christmas shopping.

Officer Caputo stopped by before lunch. My tablet and yellow pad were still on the table and he asked me what I was doing. I showed him the photos I snapped and mentioned that Uncle Ben and I were trying to see if we could predict where the next piece of window art would appear. With all of the snow on the ground now, it's unlikely we will see any sidewalk art. He looked at the images and my notes. He noted the skinny roll and said it looked like a rolled and tied diploma, and that the brown rectangle looked like a door. I wrote his suggestions down to show Uncle Ben. I think he's onto something.

I asked if he was any closer to finding out who was doing all this mysterious artwork. He admitted that his attention over the past week was focused on a variety of outdoor items that have been disappearing from local backyards. He seemed irritated with the situation so I didn't press him for any more details.

Tuesday, December 19, 2017, 10:11 AM

It feels like Christmas is right around the corner, and so it is! The heavy clouds are allowing festive lights to glow. Early this morning, George was kind enough to bring me some Christmas CDs from his little free library that Stormy donated. The CDs he brought were mainly instrumental in nature, perfect for Bailey's. I have them in the music rotation now. The clouds started shaking loose some light snow about ten minutes ago. Stormy said to expect an inch, maybe two, between today and tonight.

Uncle Ben was in a little later than usual. He arrived a few minutes after Mrs. Krumm stopped in for a few items before the school day started. He had time for a quick cup of coffee as we looked over the window art again. I told him about Officer Caputo's observations. He nodded in agreement and wondered why he didn't recognize the diploma. The brown door with "222" scribbled at the top gave yet another clue. We both started to suspect that the next window art would appear at the school. The element of specificity in the door might indicate that the next creation would occur on the window that corresponds to Room 222. As we poured over the image on my tablet, Mrs. Krumm approached with a perturbed look on her face. As we both looked up, she told us that Room 222 was hers, and that her classroom windows had better remain clean. If the artist knows what's good, he or she best pick another window. After Mrs. Krumm left with her goods, both Uncle Ben and I looked at each other and started laughing. This could be interesting.

Going through inventory with Gracie over the last few days, and trying to determine what to order for the end of the week has been exhausting. Now that the task is done, my plan is to layer up, slip on my hiking boots, and take a stroll down the Jasmine Creek footpath. Every time I immerse myself in the wintry woods, I feel like writing a follow up to Robert Frost's poem, Stopping by Woods on a Snowy Evening.

Tuesday, December 19, 2017, 8:09 PM

Less than an inch of snow freshened the ground cover today. It doesn't take much to brighten the old snow cover. While it was just enough, it didn't have any significant impact on travel. After Jennifer's homemade pizza, we all piled into the car for our nightly CLIP run. The snowy landscape seems to have brought out renewed interest in decorating. The CLIP number was 101, the highest I can remember this early in the season, and tying last year's maximum of 101 for three days either side of

Christmas Day. It will be interesting to see if we set a new record.

I'm enjoying this relatively new tradition. I was certain it was something Joel and Jessie would lose interest in after a year or two, but it is just as exciting now as it was when I discovered their very first CLIP count. I do wonder when this tradition will be shelved. I also wonder if each will do something similar with their children when that season comes. Perhaps I can facilitate this family tradition in time, telling our future grandchildren how their father and mother counted Christmas lights between two predetermined points.

Jasmine Creek was peaceful, especially with flurries effortlessly drifting out of the sky. I enjoy picking out one flake high above my head, and following it to the ground. My aim is to pick one that will end up landing into the creek where it is instantly transformed from solid to liquid. Compared to the volume of water in the creek, one little snowflake would not seem like much of a contribution. George, who has all sorts of science tidbits ready at all times, once told me that the average snowflake contains one quintillion (1,000,000,000,000,000,000) water molecules. That number is simply beyond comprehension. George also told me that the vast majority of those water molecules will take 22 days to eventually reach the mouth of the Mississippi River in the Gulf of Mexico. The water molecules that make up those snowflakes I watched disappear into the creek will be entering the Gulf of Mexico on January 10, 2018. I have no trouble imagining that God can track each individual molecule to its next destination, whether it's the Gulf, or an ice jam on the Tuscarawas, or back in the air to join another cloud. Psalm 139:6 says it best when David penned, "such knowledge is too wonderful for me, too lofty for me to attain." I could not have said it any better.

Just as I was about to turn around and return to Bailey's, I spotted something that was bright, florescent orange. It was near the base of the big maple tree. I made my way to it through the snow and found a bright orange flag, a small artist's paintbrush with red paint on it, and a couple of strands of tinsel. I'm wondering if this was the same tree where the kids found the sidewalk chalk and Uncle Ben's handkerchief. The collection was very odd until I found something else. About a foot away, a crow's feather was sticking out of the snowpack. Was this the work of Bonnie and Clyde? I've seen them around this year, but only from time to time. I brought the flag and the dainty paintbrush back to Bailey's.

The Rayburns came in after school dismissed this afternoon. They picked up a few items so that Miss Marcie could make her award-winning apple pie for the teacher's Christmas party after their students are dismissed for Christmas break. She asked if John Rowe and I would like to come and sample a sliver. I was certain that John would want to sample the pie that won the big New Year's Eve contest two years ago, so I accepted on his behalf. I asked if we might come in before the kids were dismissed so we could surround ourselves with the special joy that only comes from seeing kids excited about Christmas. I'm sure it's no different from what I recall from my years in that very same school.

I did tell Joel and Jessie that I'd be visiting their school tomorrow. Their faces had panic written all over them, but I reassured them that the main reason was to sample Mrs. Rayburn's apple pie after school let out.

Wednesday, December 20, 2017, 8:00 AM

More light snow today, about an inch. I'm glad it wasn't enough for a snow day. "Miss Miller's" pie awaits. John Rowe texted me back yesterday evening and was eager to join me in the teacher's lounge.

Many of the teachers who stopped in for coffee this morning knew that John and I would be paying them a visit this afternoon. Word spreads fast. I'm grateful that everyone expressed a genuine joy that we would be joining them for their private Christmas party. Even Mrs. Krumm knew that we would arrive early before the kid's dismissal and asked me to stop by her second grade classroom. She said she had a surprise for me. One of her delicious sugar cookies perhaps?

Uncle Ben wasn't around this morning. He said he needed to attend to some morning errands, but hoped to stop in before I closed today. Officer Caputo did stop by for a coffee to go. While I was pouring coffee into his travel mug, he spotted the fluorescent orange flag on one of the tables by the window. He said he had lost his antenna flag a few days ago. After a closer examination, he was certain it was his. I told him where I found it and also showed him the small artist's paintbrush that was found nearby. His eyes opened wide as he studied it. He asked if he could hang onto it for a while. I could see he was thinking. Perhaps this is another clue to all the artwork we've been seeing around town. It took a small paintbrush to finally pique a deeper interest in something he dismissed as "mischief" up to this point.

Jennifer and I let the kids stay up later than usual last night. Both Joel and Jessie changed into their comfy pajamas early. Jennifer and I did the same. Then together, we made a ton of popcorn drizzled with melted butter from Rich's Dairy Farm in Oxford. Three large popcorn bowls followed us to the living room where we watched the animated Christmas special, How The Grinch Stole Christmas, followed by the classic claymation film, Rudolph the Red-Nosed-Reindeer. When that was done, the fun wasn't quite over. Still in our pajamas, we all piled into the car for our late-night CLIP run. Jennifer, Joel, and Jessie all counted 102, a new record high number. I'm sure they were quite tired this morning, but with no assignments due and a half-day of school, they'll be just fine.

Wednesday, December 20, 2017, 4:55 PM

There were a number of surprises that awaited me as I pulled open the door to the school I remember so well. The first was that familiar school smell. While I remember the smell from parent-teacher night last year, I most remember it from my youthful years maneuvering its rooms and long hallways. Little has changed except for the faces and the fashions. A part of me wanted to be a kid again, to run through the halls chewing gum, screaming, and laughing. Another part of me wished I hadn't come. That was the part of me that realized this is no longer my domain. It belongs to Joel and Jessie, and their friends and classmates. My memories of those cherished school days are sweet indeed, but I will resist the temptation to relive them. They are best enjoyed as memories that are framed by the present.

Memories are funny things. I was certain I remembered the room number sequence as I moved down the long, main hallway. Have the room numbers changed since I wandered these halls many decades ago? It was unlikely, since the numbers attached to the door frames were the same markers I remember.

Once at Room 222, I turned and looked inside. Mrs. Krumm saw me and and waved me in. Her students were quietly working on some artwork. She proudly escorted me to her windows where she showed me that every single one had snowflake art painted on them. Her second graders had been hard at work this morning in a pre-emptive art strike on the risk that, based on the most recent art clues, the mysterious artist would visit her classroom windows next. It was a brilliant move! Having the window paint on the inside was also a stroke of genius.

While I could not turn back the hands of time, I did revel in the excitement of dismissal. If only we could harvest the energy I saw in the hallways as the kids bolted out of their classrooms for the beginning of Christmas break. It took no longer than ten minutes to have the school empty out and for the hallways to be largely silent.

John caught up with me in the teacher's lounge where everyone waited for Miss Marcie to dole out slices of her apple pie. John was given the first piece. After one bite, he insisted she appear on his cooking program to share her technique and recipe if she was willing. I must admit, I would have a tough time deciding which apple pie was better, Jennifer's Mt. Mansfield pie, or Miss Marcie's blue-ribbon pie. Both are outstanding.

John worked the teacher's lounge, asking everyone what their favorite foods were. He told me later that he was busy planning the big Saturday meal he was hosting at the church. He was hoping to put a fun spin on some of Pilaf's favorite foods. After pressing him about how this was going to help get my Bible study class into the habit of daily reading, he put his hand to his chin for a moment and thought. After a few seconds, he looked straight at me and said, "You'll just have to trust me."

Thursday, December 21, 2017, 7:11 AM

Thank goodness for festive Christmas lights. We've not seen any significant sunshine for a week. Between the waves of light snow and the battleship gray skies, the only color to break through what looks like a black and white photo comes from all of the Christmas lights in Pilaf. I'm grateful for living in the town that has always known how to celebrate the holidays with style and joy.

The kids went to bed early last night after an early CLIP run. The CLIP number stood at 102. Having been shorted on sleep the night before, they will quickly get back on track now that they are on Christmas break. I'd be surprised if they woke any earlier that 9 or 10 o'clock.

Thursday, December 21, 2017, 3:21 PM

Something told me not to buy into the quiet, peaceful start to the day. Up until 11:15 a.m., the biggest issue was having to order more eggnog when we ran out yesterday. All that changed when George came flying in during his mail delivery route and told us that it looked like there was new window art on one of the school windows.

Officer Caputo was at the counter having a cup of chicken soup at the time. He didn't turn around, but kept eating his soup. I suggested we all take a look. Officer Caputo stopped enjoying his soup long enough to say that he'd be right behind us, but that the artwork wasn't likely going anywhere so he wanted to finish his soup. I couldn't fault him for doing what he could to warm up before heading back out into the cold and cloudy breeze.

Uncle Ben was driving up just as George and I were heading out Bailey's front door. When we told him what was going on, he insisted on driving us so he could examine it as well. There was a gleam in his eyes and a smile on his face when he realized that, with the help of Officer Caputo, we correctly predicted where the artist would strike next.

The artwork was elaborate, taking up the length of four classroom window panes. I looked for Mrs. Krumm's snowflake designs but could not locate them. We walked up and down the west side of the school twice and found only the new window artwork. Knowing that Room 222 was smack dab in the middle of the west wing, we discovered that the new artwork was indeed painted on Mrs. Krumm's windows. Where were the snowflakes I saw yesterday?

Officer Caputo arrived. Uncle Ben, George, and I showed him to the panes where the artist had struck. I insisted that there were snowflakes painted on these windows on the inside the day before. Now they were gone. Officer Caputo took a coin out of his pocket and walked up to one of the windows. He pulled out his readers and tried scraping some of the paint off with the coin, but he could not. That's when he told us that this was, quite literally, an inside job. Apparently, someone washed Mrs. Krumm's snowflakes off the window, and painted the new design on the inside. Whoever did this had easy access to the school after it was secured for Christmas break.

Officer Caputo wanted a closer look. Since he has keys to virtually every building in town, he suggested we go inside for a closer look.

Once inside Mrs. Krumm's second grade classroom, the detail in the window art popped. It was much easier to see once backlit from the overcast skies. I snapped many photos to look at closely on my tablet tomorrow. The number right in the middle of the artwork was "102." That was our

CLIP number. Joel and Jessie insist they've not been telling anyone about their Christmas light count. Then how did the artist know?

After I took plenty of photos to examine later, Uncle Ben and I leaned only a few whiskers away from being able to see the detail in the artwork. It looked like a storyboard that went from left to right. On the left, a group of people of various ages were all headed to the right. The next window pane had doors with arrows pointing inside a building. The third window pane had a man in a chef's toque overseeing a number of pots steaming on a stove. The final window pane depicted a large easel with a painting of what appeared to be a book painted on it. The date "December 23" was written above the easel.

We didn't need Officer Caputo's help with this one. Both Uncle Ben and I agreed that the next piece of artwork would appear at John Rowe's special dinner on Saturday night, perhaps on an easel. Officer Caputo pointed to the easel and was about to say something. After a few seconds, he waved his thought away and motioned for us to head out the door with him.

Friday, December 22, 2017, 9:28 AM

We finally had a short window of sunshine just after sunrise. The clouds were quick to return and so were the snow showers. Stormy was busy tracking heavy lake effect snow up in the snowbelt. Our snow showers are simply their leftovers, but enough to keep the landscape looking like Christmas.

Uncle Ben stopped in around 7 o'clock. He looked tired. He did mention that all this investigative analysis with the mysterious artwork was getting old and exhausting. I have to agree. Assuming we figured things out correctly, it's a wait and see game now.

Mrs. Krumm stopped in to give me one of her sugar cookies. She remembered that I liked them and saved one for me. I stuck to the apple pie in the teacher's lounge when we were there two days ago. The apple pie filled my belly and squashed my appetite for anything else that was offered, including Mrs. Krumm's cookies.

I asked her if she had seen the new artwork that replaced her painted snowflakes. I did not expect her reaction. Not only was Mrs. Krumm not upset, but she even thought that the windows looked far better than what she did in her preemptive strike.

Officer Caputo ran in for coffee. He was in a hurry, but he did stop to chat with Mrs. Krumm for a moment. I assume it was related to the window art in her room. Both were smiling and chuckling. It seems to me that both should be much more upset than what they are outwardly projecting. Either Uncle Ben and I are physically exhausted and mentally clouded more than when we realize, or this town has simply gone mad.

Friday, December 22, 2017, 5:55 PM

Finally... it's crystal clear, but it sure is cold outside. I let the wood stove go out an hour ago. It doesn't take long for the wintry drafts to find their way into the store. On nights like this, it would be tempting to use Bailey's as an ice cream storage facility. Then again, the ice cream stored here would outlive its expiration date. I don't bother keeping much ice cream on hand in the winter. About the only time I pull out my standby carton of vanilla ice cream is when a customer asks for a scoop on top of a warmed slice of apple pie.

I had a delightful day once I set aside the mental gymnastics of trying to figure out who the secret artist is, and how they apparently discovered Joel and Jessie's CLIP number. As often as customers would bring it up, I would simply shrug my shoulders and talk instead about how delightfully Christmasy the weather has been.

George stopped by and asked me if I had any outgoing mail. I actually did, but I told him I wanted to walk up to the post office to get some fresh air and exercise. As someone who walks several miles a day for his job, George understood. There's something about a leisure walk that does a phenomenal job of vacuuming up mind clutter.

I was leaving the store under Gracie's command when the dairy truck from Rich's came by with the extra eggnog. I'm confident that what we ordered will be out the door by closing time tomorrow. In fact, there were two customers in the store waiting for the eggnog to arrive.

My stroll to the post office placed the exclamation point on my deliberate effort to conduct an uncomplicated day. I took in many deep breaths of fresh, December air. It smelled clean and crisp. There was a hint of pine scent in the air from time to time. After dropping off my outgoing mail at the post office, I walked past John and Eloise's place. Instead of thinking about how their decorations looked inexplicably identical to what I witnessed with the kids two years ago, I simply stopped for a moment to admire them. You could still see their glow despite the brilliant, blue sky.

Christmas in Pilaf. I love this time of year.

Saturday, December 23, 2017, 6:57 AM

I woke just before 4 o'clock this morning. Normally, I roll over on my other side and fall back to sleep. This time, sleep would not come. Instead of thrashing around and waking Jennifer, I wandered downstairs and checked on the temperature with a small LED flashlight that Jennifer keeps near the window. It was +3°F. Still not feeling sleepy, I turned the deck light on and sat in the recliner. Sammy emerged from somewhere and sat patiently by my feet. He stared at me for the longest time as if he was asking what the problem was. Not until I told him that I just wasn't sleepy did he finally jump up on my lap, never missing an opportunity to share some warmth a cold night.

Not wanting to waste this sleepless window, I asked the Lord if there was someone needing prayer. My Bible study class came to mind. I prayed for all of us, myself included, for a renewed appetite for desiring time with Him, in prayer, in worship, and in His Word. I also prayed for Chef John. I have no idea how he purposes to use a catered meal to draw more people to God's Word, but after getting to know John and Eloise, I know their hearts. It's the good soil of Mark 4:8. I'm praying for a good harvest.

I was surprised to find Sammy and myself in the same position several hours later. My sleep was sound and I woke refreshed, ready for Bailey's last day of business before closing for Christmas Eve and Christmas Day. I'll open again at 11 o'clock Tuesday morning.

My weather station at Bailey's recorded a morning low of 0°F. With an official record low of -6°F at Akron-Canton, and -7°F at Hopkins Airport, our zero is still far away from a probable contemporary record of about -12°F to -14°F for Pilaf. I'll have to see about becoming a cooperative observer for the National Weather Service. I hear I can program my weather station to tie into a network of backyard observers called Mesonet. There's a bit more interest in our little town now that a famous chef lives here.

Saturday, December 23, 2017, 4:00 PM

Bailey's doors are locked after a steady stream of customers. One half-gallon of eggnog remains. That one is coming home with me in about 30 minutes. Gracie kept up with our closing list so that I would not have a lot to do when I locked the doors behind her. I'll see her at the John Rowe dinner tonight at the church hall.

It was great seeing the sunshine make an all-day appearance. I was beginning to think Pilaf had moved into the snowbelt or the mountains of northern New England where sunshine can be a rare commodity in the winter months. High clouds are arriving as I write this. That usually means a glamorous sunset, full of deep colors. We're all counting on the Christmas Eve snow that Stormy talked about on the radio yesterday.

No one that I know has seen John Rowe anywhere today. Makes sense. He's preparing something special for a lot of people tonight. I can't imagine cooking for a hundred guests. Jennifer and

I are lucky to pull off a holiday meal for a dozen without something going awry.

Sunday, December 24, 2017, 7:00 AM

Some Christmas Eves are slow and peaceful. That was last year. The downside was having no snow on the ground. The air wasn't cold and fresh. In fact, it was almost 70°F the day after Christmas! I felt bad for the kids who got skis and snowboards. There really wasn't anywhere to go to try them out unless you drove into New York state. Even there, the conditions were not exactly ideal. Joel and Jessie's CLIP runs became more of a mundane routine. Hitting a CLIP record of 101 should have excited them more. I was certain I would not see a resurrection of the CLIP runs this year. I'm glad I was wrong.

Fast-forward to 2017. It's a completely different ball game. For starters, the snow arrived. Once here, it remained. The atmosphere has seen to its maintenance by adding to it little-by-little. Thanks to George's music little free library and a generous radio meteorologist, Pilaf has been treated to an expanded selection of Christmas music. And to make life even more exciting, Pilaf has been pulled into two dramas that have eclipsed everything else happening in our little town. Those two dramas collided head-on in a way none of us expected last night.

It was a high-fashion night at the church fellowship hall. We arrived early enough to see it fill up from nearly empty to brimming with people dressed for a special event. There were sharp tuxes, flowing gowns, three-piece suits, and glittery dresses. The tables were set with fine china and stemware. Each table had a cluster of festive Christmas candles. A captivating aroma wafted from the kitchen and permeated every corner. There was a lectern near the closed kitchen door, but it was the object to the right of the lectern that grabbed my attention. What appeared to be a very large easel was covered by a deep red, velvety drape. As soon as I saw it, I looked for Uncle Ben. He must have spotted it at the same time as we both quickly moved to meet each other. An easel. Food. People gathering. Could this be the next clue? Was John so busy in the kitchen that he didn't see this being brought in? Why was it covered? We both so desperately wanted to peek under the drape, but there were too many eyes that would have witnessed our nosiness.

John emerged from the kitchen with a full staff of chefs to much applause. He stepped up to the lectern and asked everyone to find their place. He made no reference to the easel. Surely he must have seen it. It was like the elephant in the room, but no one dared ask him about it.

He announced that tonight's meal would come in four courses. The first was an amuse bouche, an appetizer served to prepare the guest for the other courses. The term is a French phrase which literally means "mouth amuser." There were ten chefs serving each of the ten tables, delivering a tall stemmed glass with a frothy liquid, with layers of deep orange and cream. Chef John explained that it was a warmed whipped pumpkin soup with coriander creme fraiche and sesame crisp. It was so delicious that if the meal would have stopped there, not a single person would have minded. But there was so much more. Just when we thought our taste buds hit a pinnacle, the next course brought us higher. It was an epicurean's dream dinner. Chef John hit a grand slam home run. When he reemerged from the kitchen with his team of chefs as we were finishing our meal, we all stood to show him our love and appreciation.

After he motioned us to be seated, with a deep smile, he looked at each table, then spoke. He said nothing about the meal. Instead he moved to the covered easel. He told us that under the drape was some artwork from the artist who has been leaving sidewalk and window art all over town in the last few weeks. The murmurs began. I could see Officer Caputo suddenly paying close attention.

Chef John said that in one week, we were all invited back to the same table for another dinner during which he would reveal the mysterious artist. Then he uncovered the easel. We were all free to examine the new piece. He also said that there would be a new one brought in every day. It will be placed in the church classroom. Anyone who wanted to stop by to examine it was welcomed to do so during the day, not just those who partook in tonight's meal. While Dr. O'Connor did not know the identity of the artist, he did agree to host the daily artwork in the large church classroom. It was easy to see why. Instead of a number in the middle, there was a Bible reference. It was Psalm 119.

Chef John then said goodnight and disappeared into the kitchen. Officer Caputo quickly followed him there, I'm certain to question him. Everyone else started looking at the colorful artwork.

This has been such a crazy December that I can't imagine compounding it with any more drama. Yet, I sense we've not yet reached the summit.

It's still dark. No snow is falling yet, but there's still plenty on the ground. Our outdoor lights look grand. Sammy is curled up next to me on the couch, occasionally asking me to put my laptop down so I can scratch him under the chin and watch him smile and purr. How can I say no? The focus shift serves as a great relaxation method.

Sunday, December 24, 2017, 4:25 PM

I love it when Christmas Eve falls on a Sunday. The church is full for both the usual Sunday morning service and the Christmas Eve service, which is tonight at 6 o'clock.

Our Bible study class was also well-attended. The giant easel and artwork from yesterday was tucked in the front right corner. As if planned, one of the ceiling lights flooded the artwork to make it the room's primary center of attention. Since it was Christmas Eve, we simply read Luke Chapter 2 together, then enjoyed some of the coffee and pastries that Jimmy Giammalvo provided. There were a couple of new people that came. Since they heard about the new artwork on display here, they spent most of their time looking it over and discussing its meaning. A few of them asked for a Bible to look up Psalm 119. Dr. O'Connor sensed they didn't own one and insisted they take the ones he brought into the classroom earlier. Most of them stayed for the worship service, too. If this is what it took to get people to open up such a precious Book, then I'm on board. But who is the artist, and how did all this get started? While the CLIP number is no longer in the center, how was it obtained for the sidewalk and window art? Joel & Jessie still claim they told no one.

A slow, Charlie Brown snow started falling from the sky about a half-hour ago. It's not the kind that causes a problem on the roads, so the church should be packed for the candlelight service.

Last night's meal from Chef John was amazing, but I would never trade it for the home-cooked meal Jennifer planned for our family after church. The aroma coming from the kitchen is marvelous. There's something in the crock pot and Jennifer shooed me out of the kitchen when I tried to take a peek. I'll have to wait, drool and all. George and Gracie are coming over to join us after church. Knowing whose birth it is we celebrate tonight makes my joy complete.

Monday, December 25, 2017, 5:57 AM

A ray of heaven kissed Pilaf last night. When that happens, nothing can steal the joy and peace that falls upon mankind. It was as if the angels greeted us with the same tidings they gave the shepherds over two millennia ago.

"Glory to God in the highest, and on earth peace, good will toward men."

We all arrived with broad smiles and a sugar coating of snow on our heads and coats. The lights were low and soft in the sanctuary as we sang of the love that drove God's Son to come in the flesh to rescue us from our sin. We sang my favorite, Cantique De Noël, better known as O, Holy Night. Dr. O'Connor touched the essence of God's love for us in his Christmas Eve devotional in a way that made heaven more real than anything we know or can experience on planet Earth. He made us yearn for it, wanting to be in that place beyond description where God's light fills everything. It's a place where there are no shadows, no darkness, no sorrow, no death. Heaven truly kissed us.

Pilaf has surely seen its share of commotion in the last few weeks, but not a single soul seemed to think about any of it. I know full well that the peace that transcends human understanding is never a function of location, but somehow I get the sense that the peace we have here in Pilaf would be difficult to find anywhere else.

There are still flurries in the air. Three inches of new snow last night promises to give Pilaf a Courier and Ives look as we say hello to Christmas Day.

Jennifer was up before me. The smell of breakfast will soon stir the kids. Oh, yes. It's Christmas Day. Praise God, it's Christmas Day.

Monday, December 25, 2017, 7:43 PM

Such a peaceful day. The snow stopped around 11 o'clock this morning. The sun began to take over in the afternoon. There wasn't much melting, though. It stayed in the low 20s with a breeze occasionally blowing tufts of snow off the roof.

We had a couple of small, collectible gifts waiting for Joel and Jessie after breakfast, but we decided very early on that our big Christmas gift would be an overnight family trip to the new Noah's Ark exhibit in Williamstown, Kentucky, with a second day at the Creation Museum just outside Cincinnati. To prepare ourselves for this journey, we did purchase a DVD pack that explains various aspects of the ark, as well as how the replica was built. That was the one big gift we let the kids unwrap together. We already watched one of the DVDs this afternoon.

Jim's family stopped over for a few hours this afternoon. The cousins had a blast together building a snow fort in the backyard. How they managed to get the powdery snow to stick well enough to accomplish what they did is beyond me. We invited them to stay for dinner, but they decided to head home as it was getting dark.

Because everyone was up early, I took Joel and Jessie on their CLIP run right after dinner. We have a new record set at 107! I think the snow helped Pilaf decorate this year. Will "107" show up on the easel art anytime this week? I honestly don't know how that's possible. I guess we'll find out this week at the church.

Tuesday, December 26, 2017, 5:52 AM

I told Gracie to enjoy the day off today. The day after Christmas is usually pretty quiet. There's no reason to believe this year will be any different. That's why I was up at five. Maureen Whittles was here ten minutes ago with my morning pastries from Giammalvo's Market. The order was smaller, but not as small as the day after Thanksgiving. I typically see only a few goodies sell on the day after Thanksgiving. People don't seem to get as stuffed on Christmas Day compared to Thanksgiving. My guess is that Uncle Ben will still grab his usual cherry Danish though.

The stars were brilliant, and the air cold and calm this morning. Even though I stepped inside the store to turn on a few lights and turn up the heat, I was still drawn back outside. I stood just beyond the porch where I had a great view of the northern and eastern sky. The Big Dipper is so easy to spot, riding almost overhead. Cassiopeia, the constellation that looks like a giant "W," is so low in the northern sky that it's barely visible above the bare trees north of Bailey's. Orion has set, making most of its night run in the Christmas evening sky now. I saw what seemed like a low-orbiting satellite heading north. George tells me there are quite a few of them visible. You can tell the difference between satellites and aircraft by determining whether the lights blink or if they are steady. If they blink, it's an aircraft. If it's steady, it's a satellite.

The air was so still and quiet that it seemed as if I could hear the stars sing. God humorously asked Job if he was there during creation when the "all stars sang together" in Job Chapter 38. Figurative? Maybe. But maybe not! They may sing in a frequency our ears are not designed to pick up.

Tuesday, December 26, 2017, 7:00 PM

Our family just returned from stopping by the church to see the new artwork. Earlier today, the news spread quickly. The Bailey's buzz was that it was on display in the adult classroom, just as Chef John promised. Even Gary Bittner mentioned it on his afternoon radio program on WPLF.

None of us can remember the church parking lot so busy on a Tuesday. Dr. O'Connor was in the classroom attending to new visitors who were unfamiliar with the layout of the church. They came driven by sheer curiosity. Some of the visitors left with new Bibles in their hands. Some did not. The universal comment was how the artwork was so colorful and meticulously detailed.

The Psalm 119 text in the center of the first piece was now at the very top. There was a simple number "11" in the center, surrounded by rainbows, clouds, and human eyes on the top, and what looked like a large page with unreadable text below the number. The color turned to an ominous black below the page. I could only assume that the meaning of the artwork was embedded in Verse 11. Jennifer pulled out her smartphone and read Psalm 119:11 to us.

"I have hidden your word in my heart that I might not sin against you."

Dr. O'Connor told me how often this same scene repeated, sometimes from people he never expected to open up God's Word.

I had the chance to pull Dr. O'Connor aside at one point and asked him if he knew the identity of the artist. While he loved to pull a nonsensical prank every once in awhile, he has always been truthful with everyone. He looked me straight in the eye and said he did not know. He could only guess, but that my guess was as good as anyone else's. While a huge mystery remains, Dr. O'Connor was choosing to focus on the renewed interest in the Scriptures. I'm glad he shared that. I found myself suddenly excited about having a full Bible study classroom with attentive hearts and minds this Sunday.

Wednesday, December 27, 2017, 10:10 AM

Gracie opened the store today. I had a delightful morning enjoying breakfast with Jennifer, Joel, and Jessie. While we were having a traditional breakfast together, I looked over by the coat rack and saw the pile of school books that Jessie left under our coats was still there. It was the same pile I asked her to move to her room at the end of last week. I drew in a measured breath to temper my displeasure before I spoke. That's when I saw something that made me stop cold.

I excused myself from the table and started walking over to the books. Jessie saw what was happening and began to profusely apologize for not moving the books. I assured her it was something she could take care of after breakfast.

I took the book at the top of the pile in my hands. It was her math book. It was covered in the usual brown paper book cover with an array of little

drawings and other cute artifacts. What caught my
attention was a list of numbers near the book's
middle edge. There were two columns of numbers,
ascending in value. Some of them looked very
familiar. Numbers like 17, 32, 59, 93, 101, and the
last one, 107.

I returned to the table with the book. Jessie
looked like she was going to cry. I reassured her
that I was not upset. Instead, I was very, very
interested in these written numbers on the book
cover. Jessie said that's where she had been writing
down the CLIP number after every evening's count.
She ran out of space and started a second column. I
asked her if anyone else at school asked her what
these numbers were. She said no. Then I asked if
there was anyone at school she could think of that
had an unusual interest in her math book. At first,
she said no. Then she uttered the words "except
maybe...."

Jessie told me that virtually every school day,
Mrs. Krumm, the second grade teacher stopped by
her homeroom to say good morning. The only row
she would visit was where Jessie was seated. Math
was Jessie's first class, so most of the time, that's the
book that was on top, ready to go. She thought it
was odd that the second grade teacher was coming
to say hello to all of the seventh graders in a
completely different part of the building.

Could Mrs. Krumm be the mystery artist?
Wasn't it Officer Caputo who suspected an inside job

when the window art was found on the inside of her classroom windows? It's a reasonable conclusion, but for a lot or reasons, I just can't buy that story. I'm guessing this is only a big clue that will lead to something else and something bigger. I just know it.

Officer Caputo came in about an hour ago. It was my intention to inform him of my morning discovery, but something didn't look right. I couldn't place my finger on it. Usually calm and steady, there was a hint of panic on his face that went beyond the rosy cheeks from the brisk air. He was looking around Bailey's floor, under tables, and under chairs. Uncle Ben greeted him with a joyful hello, but he barely acknowledged him with a half-smile and a wave.

He finally came over and asked me if anyone had seen his officer's badge, the one he often wears near his side pocket on a belt clip. I scanned his belt. That's what didn't look right. There was no badge. I had to tell him no, but that I would give Bailey's a careful sweep before the lunch crowd arrived. I promised to call him immediately if I found it.

Wednesday, December 27, 2017, 6:38 PM

No badge. I texted Officer Caputo after an unusually heavy lunch crowd so that he would know.

All of our cream soups have been particularly popular this month. I'm convinced the lovely Christmas snowscape has a lot to do with it. I made a cream of mushroom with a hint of tarragon and thyme. The blackboard special paired it up with a corned beef and Swiss on buttered, rye toast. The only rye bread I had remaining after the lunch rush were the two slices closest to the nubby stub. Not being able to make a sandwich with it, and having seen Bonnie and Clyde in the parking lot, I walked out on the porch and tossed it to Pilaf's mischievous resident crows. I expected them to fly away, but they watched as I tossed them the bread. They wasted no time hopping to the bread and tearing it apart to gobble it up. Made me smile. I've seen them hanging out a little more in recent days. George claims they've been flying down toward the Jasmine Creek quite a bit. We have been finding a few interesting items by the base of the big maple tree. I should take a walk to the creek tomorrow. Perhaps there are a few new goodies there.

I'm getting ready to head back home. Clean up took a while, even with Gracie's help. I'm glad Neil and Dawn Manausa came in for lunch today since I never had the chance to run to the church and see the new artwork. I knew I could count on Neil to have photos on his smart tablet. Not only did he snap a photo of the entire easel, but he snapped some interesting close-ups with details that a casual eye may have overlooked.

Psalm 119 still overshadowed the new piece at the very top. The number 37 showed up in the middle this time. There was an inner circle of objects and an outer ring of bright, rainbow colors and light rays. Neil's close ups of the inner circle revealed some interesting elements. The first thing I noticed was the pronounced swirl of red, the kind of red that screams of caution. Swirling inside the sea of red were computers, smartphones, game stations, gold coins, an expensive sports car, footballs, baseballs, movie tickets, a television, a cruise ship, and several palm trees. Neil said these were just a handful of the items meticulously depicted within the inner ring.

Dawn encouraged me to read Verse 37 of Psalm 119. It's something they had already done at the church. They were confident I would understand the meaning behind the two circles after reading the passage.

"Turn my eyes from worthless things, and give me life through your word."

It made me examine those items in the inside ring that stood in the way of the bright rainbow ring on the outside. How can any of us hope to break through so much worldly distraction? Neil grabbed his Bible and looked down on it. He didn't need to say it, but he did for the benefit of allowing his own ears to hear his declaration, "By staying in His Word daily." I could not agree more.

Dawn said that there was a constant flow of people coming into the church to examine today's canvas. It seems like more and more people are coming each day.

Thursday, December 28, 2017, 10:56 AM

Stormy called for a little rain or wet snow later this afternoon, so I took an hour or so to take a walk down the Jasmine Creek footpath a while ago. The snowpack has better traction now that temperatures have moderated. It was 34°F on my weather station at Bailey's before I took my walk. Factor in no wind, and it felt relatively balmy compared to the last week or two.

Since the air was so cold for a few weeks leading to Christmas, the creek was mostly ice and snow covered. There are still many places in the middle where open water is bubbling out. It takes a long, cold winter to freeze the Jasmine Creek completely. The last time I saw that happen was my first year back in Pilaf as the owner of Bailey's. There wasn't much ice on the creek at all last winter, so finding this wintry scene was a peaceful gift.

As I approached the base of the big maple tree where I found Officer Caputo's orange antenna flag, I heard Bonnie and Clyde's call. They swooped down for a landing. Perfect timing. They didn't seem to mind that I was approaching them. Perhaps they thought I was going toss them some more rye bread. They remained at the tree base guarding something until I reached about ten paces. Now too close for comfort, they cackled and cawed as they took to the sky. I could now see the stash they were collecting.

Among the random objects, there was another artist's paintbrush. It was caked with dried, red paint. A cheeseburger wrapper was motionless by the tree's roots. Had there been any wind, that wrapper would be elsewhere by now. Something told me to move it out of the way. I'm glad I listened to that silent voice. As I moved the wrapper, there it was. Officer Caputo's belt badge. It looked as though it had been dragged through some of the red paint on the artist's paintbrush. Surely the badge's luster could be restored, but more importantly, it will be returned to its rightful owner.

I just texted him with the good news. I've not received a return text or call yet, but I know it won't take long.

Thursday, December 28, 2017, 10:37 PM

It's raining lightly tonight. The afternoon clouds did shake loose a few wet snowflakes, but by dark, the intermittent light rain took over. The car thermometer depicted 39°F as we all piled in to drive around and admire the Christmas lights. The rain wasn't heavy enough to remove the snowpack that firmly held onto the Pilaf landscape, so everyone was okay with the rain. The raindrops on the front windshield and side windows added a glittering effect to many of the lights. We made only one CLIP pass from Bailey's to our house. There was no need to double-count the steady-state of Christmas week. The CLIP number is happily holding at 107 and will probably stay there until sometime next week.

Despite the short work week, each day has had a long and draining feel. So much is going on in town that staying on top of the latest headlines has been challenging. Admittedly, I don't like having to tell Bailey's visitors that I don't know the mystery artist's identity. I suppose I could pretend to know, then zip my lips as if I hold a special secret, but that would be deceiving. The identity will be revealed in about 44 hours. Chef John is the only one privy to such things. I've not been successful in pulling anything significant out of him.

The unlikely trio of Uncle Ben, Neil Manausa, and Mrs. Krumm was huddled around the items I found on the Jasmine Creek footpath early this afternoon. They were at the end of the lunch counter. Uncle Ben observed that the shade of red on the badge matched the overall color of the inner ring in yesterday's artwork at the church. Mrs. Krumm held the paintbrush in her hand. I made the mistake of telling her that she was a natural holding that paintbrush. She gently put the paintbrush down, then proceeded to shake her finger at me.

"Danny Rice, don't you even begin to think for a second that I had anything to do with all that crazy artwork. If I hear you've been entertaining that silly notion, you won't get a single sugar cookie from me next Christmas."

Duly noted.

Officer Caputo finally showed up a few hours before Bailey's closed. I expected him much earlier since his response to my text was relatively quick. He thanked me for finding his badge and was quite relieved when he saw it. The red paint startled him, but he seemed confident he could remove it without too much effort. When I showed him the paintbrush I found nearby, he examined it closely and asked me if he could take it. I had no objection. What in the world would I do with a used artist's paintbrush caked with red paint? I'm sure it's more evidence to Officer Caputo. He left before I had the chance to ask him if he was able to pry any worthwhile information out of Chef John.

Despite feeling a bit weary, I did stop by the church on the way home to see today's artwork. It seems like more and more people are coming as we approach the weekend. I saw a number of people I have not seen in a long time. These canvases have certainly captured the attention of Pilaf.

The number 105 was at the center. Had it been 107, I might have been tempted to think that the CLIP number had returned. Psalm 119 is not only the longest Psalm in the Bible, it's also the longest chapter anywhere in the Scriptures at 176 verses.

Verse 105 says, "Your word is a lamp for my feet, and a light for my path."

Friday, December 29, 2017, 8:52 AM

The icy fingers of old man winter made a fist and slammed it right back into Pilaf while we slept. Stormy did warn us. The brief thaw was going to be a one-day affair. He made it sound so poetic on the radio that it may have distracted from the reality of waking up to single-digit temperatures and below-zero wind chills. As arctic as everything looked during my quick drive to Bailey's, it still warmed my spirit to see the expressions of Christmas all over town. Even the Pilaf Credit Union's sign, usually overloaded with interest rate advertisements, is still blinking a red-and-green "Merry Christmas."

The lock on the front door of Bailey's, despite the warmth of my soul, was solidly frozen. There was probably just enough wind to push some of yesterday's rain into the lock. This morning's freeze must have happened very quickly for that water to have frozen the lock shut. Fortunately, the lock on the side door cooperated. That gave me the time I needed to locate the spray I use to solve such issues before I opened the store. The problem was finding it. Last winter was so warm, I never used it. It was tucked away behind all of my tools. Neil Manausa tried to convince me to replace my old lock with a keyless pad last year. If he walks in the door this morning, I'll have him order me one.

Customers coming through the door today all had several things in common. Most were unrecognizable through the layers upon layers of winter attire, and most looked thirty pounds or more heavier than their normal weight. It's no surprise that I didn't recognize George when he initially came through the door. His mail delivery bag was the only thing that gave him away. He was actually looking for Uncle Ben. He hoped that he could get his help opening up his music little free library. The door was iced shut. I gave him my lock de-icing spray and told him about my adventure trying to get into the store.

Dr. O'Connor was next. He, too, was looking for Uncle Ben. In response, I asked him if the church door locks were frozen. He asked me how I knew. He didn't believe it was a lucky guess.

Eloise Rowe was no more than five minutes behind Dr. O'Connor. She had been waiting for him to open the door at the church so she could bring in the new artwork. There were more than a dozen customers inside Bailey's who suddenly fell silent, their heads whipping around to see if Eloise had the new canvas. I went for broke. I asked Eloise if we could see it before she brought it to the church. If she didn't show us, no loss. If she did, Bailey's would be the talk of the town instead of being the place where everyone talks about the town.

She first looked at Dr. O'Connor. He shrugged his shoulders and didn't see any harm in it.

Bailey's lit up as this final piece of artwork was unveiled right in the middle of the open space. Like all the others, Psalm 119 was bannered at the top. There was an elaborate buffet table shaped like a giant, upside down U. The number "1" was to the left of the table, the number "0" inside the table, and a "3" to the right of the table. There was every kind of great food on that table. The people who gathered around it looked like people we know all too well. Uncle Ben, Harry Buser, George, Jennifer and the kids, Jim's family, Mrs. Krumm, the Rayburns, and so many others. It looked like a giant party. There was a kitchen door propped open on the upper right through which beams of brilliant light illuminated the scene. It was clear that the light in the scene came from no other source.

On the upper left, there was a concealed booth with an easel poking out from the top. You could see the top of a head and a hand painting on the canvas. The top of the canvas was visible. On the left, smeared snowflakes with a cloth in the painter's left hand. On the right, the number "222" being painted by his right hand. Assuming the mystery artist was painting himself in that position, then it could not be Mrs. Krumm. She was depicted sitting down at the table eating what looked like one of her sugar cookies. The artist in the booth appeared to be a man.

The clues from within the booth pointed back to Mrs. Krumm's second grade classroom windows.

Could it be another teacher in the school? Perhaps principal Rayburn? Officer Caputo did say it had to be an inside job.

The detail in this particular piece was stunning. Even the most accomplished artist could not have designed this in one sitting. It was certainly meant to be the artistic culmination of this entire mysterious exercise.

First, I thanked Eloise for letting us see it first. The crowds were getting pretty thick at the church, so now we won't have to fight the crowd flow. Second, I dared asked if she knew the identity of the artist. She said that John would not tell her so that she would not be pressured by anyone. Made sense.

I turned my attention back to the number in the middle. I opened my smartphone and called up Psalm 119:103 and read it out loud to everyone.

"How sweet are your words to my taste, sweeter than honey to my mouth!"

Of course! Tomorrow night's follow-up dinner.

The piece was so stunning, no one wanted to see it go, but the time had come to bring it to the church for all to see.

Friday, December 29, 2017, 7:44 PM

The cold winds never let up today. As often as I stoked the wood stove in the center of Bailey's, the cold drafts from the front door opening and closing dealt the winning hand. I was sporting my heavy, wool Christmas sweater all day. When the last lunch customer left, there was one cup of creamy clam chowder remaining. I claimed it for myself. I may have had to scrape everything from the bottom of the warming pan, but it was delicious. That's my third consecutive cream soup day. Tomorrow will be number four, a new soup record for Bailey's. Gracie already started making the base for her corn chowder. The word is already out.

I drove past the church on the way home after locking up Bailey's for the night. There was actually a modest line coming out the front door. The interest in the artwork is certainly impressive given the bitterly cold wind chill temperatures.

Chef John wasn't visible anywhere today. Eloise said he went into the city for a production meeting. That guy never stops!

Saturday, December 30, 2017, 9:22 AM

George came in this morning with a few new Christmas CDs from his little free library. He joined Uncle Ben, Officer Caputo, and me at the counter. George said that after Stormy Windham's generous donation, passers-by not only took, but left Christmas CDs to share. I gave him a handful to return to the box and took the new ones for Bailey's CD player. I asked George what he was going to do with the box after the Christmas season was over. He wasn't sure since Uncle Ben cut the box to hold music CDs, so converting it to a traditional book little free library would be difficult. Everyone who was there suggested keeping it filled with music of all kinds outside the Christmas season.

The Rayburns walked in for a few supplies while we were hanging out by the counter. Uncle Ben looked straight at Mr. Rayburn. Uncle Ben didn't have to say a word. You could see that he suspected that Mr. Rayburn was the covert artist. I have to admit, I was beginning to think the same thing until Officer Caputo tapped Uncle Ben on the shoulder to get him to turn around. Officer Caputo then leaned over to all three of us and told us that Mr. Rayburn is not the artist. He must be hot on the trail of someone else.

Officer Caputo told us he couldn't say much more, then asked us not to let on that we even had this conversation. Besides, Chef John promised to reveal the identity of the artist tonight at the church.

Saturday, December 30, 2017, 4:05 PM

For as crazy-busy as our lunch hour was, it feels like Pilaf is a ghost town right now. The shadows are exceedingly long, the air is glowing a deep yellow-orange with pink hues, and I haven't seen a soul since the last customer left over thirty minutes ago with an armful of goods. I closed early when I saw the town rolling up its sidewalk. That's one of the wonderful benefits of owning your own business.

Earlier today, we had a counter full of family for lunch. Jennifer brought Joel and Jessie, and brother Jim and Barb came with their brood, Sarah, Drake, and Vicki. They all came for Gracie's corn chowder. Everyone thought a lighter lunch would be best in preparation for tonight's presentation by Chef John and his team. I'm glad they came in before the lunch crowd hit. We ran out of corn chowder by 12:45 p.m. I had some tomato bisque ready as a back-up. While there were a few takers, there were just as many who were disappointed enough to order something entirely different. Perhaps I ought to look into marketing Gracie's corn chowder beyond Bailey's. I'll have to talk to Chef John about it sometime.

Those who came in and were on the guest list for tonight's meal had an interesting air of anticipation, a kind of giddiness that was bubbling just under the surface of their conversations. Once more, I have not seen John at all today. I'm sure he is planning to be on his best game tonight. Beating last Saturday's meal is going to be a very high bar to clear. I'm beginning to see the connection he is drawing between food and the Bible thanks to yesterday's verse on the last canvas, however, I am clueless on how he plans to pull it all together.

Sunday, December 31, 2017, 7:01 AM

Pilaf is stunned on many different levels. Where do I even begin to describe the events that rendered last evening's dinner guests speechless? A chronology of events is probably the best way to proceed.

When we arrived, the tables were all meticulously set just as they were last week. The one difference was that every place had a sterling silver domed cover over each plate. Upon entering, we were instructed to find our way to the same table and place we were assigned one week ago.

The lectern was in the same place, but to the left of it, just as it was depicted in the last piece of artwork, there was a booth concealed by a thick, white drape. The easel holding a large canvas was slightly visible from the booth's open top. The revelation of the mystery artist had been staged for the guests. I looked around for Officer Caputo. He was a few tables away. His gaze was fixed on the canvas and he appeared deep in thought.

Every chair was occupied. The conversation was lively and electric. Everyone was expecting Chef John to emerge from the kitchen at any moment. Much to everyone's surprise, a visibly shorter silhouette emerged from the bright lights as the kitchen door opened. It was Mrs. Krumm. As she moved to the lectern to take her role as the evening's master of ceremony, her nose barely cleared its lip. As the conversation lulled, there were a few giggles as Mrs. Krumm shrugged her shoulders when she could not reach the microphone. The Maître D' scrambled over with a food crate for her to stand on so she could be seen and reach the mic.

As the room grew silent, she welcomed everyone and announced that Chef John would be out soon. The first order of business was to reveal this evening's final canvas painting. Mrs. Krumm grabbed the drape and with one swift pull, cleanly yanked it off the booth like David Copperfield would have done! The artwork portrayed a big, family Bible opened in the middle highlighting 2 Timothy 3:16-17. Since Mrs. Krumm was initially silent, clearly awaiting the crowd's reaction, I joined many guests in concluding that she must be the artist.

Mrs. Krumm was quick to extinguish that thought when she said she was far too vertically challenged to have reached all of those windows in the last few weeks. As she stepped off the food crate and lifted her hands as a demonstration, the whole room erupted in laughter.

Mrs. Krumm returned to her crate at the lectern and said, "The artist you are seeking is seated among you tonight. Would you like to know who it is?"

At this point, everyone began looking around the room trying to deduce who it might be. After all the head-turning and vocal speculation stopped, Mrs. Krumm said, "Will the real mystery artist please stand up."

Various people in the crowd started standing up and sitting down, clearly to allow the drama to build. Everyone was smiling with anticipation. Suddenly, everyone sat down. Then, to everyone's amazement, one guest slowly pushed his seat back and stood tall. It was.... Officer Caputo! There was an audible gasp throughout the room. No wonder he always seemed so close to cracking the case, but never quite got there. In the end, and as Officer Caputo himself once said, it was an inside job! Very few people knew he had a hidden talent for painting, either. He kept it a closely guarded secret. He received a standing ovation for his detailed work.

So how does a police officer become such a great artist? He took to the lectern and explained that, for years, he found himself doodling and drawing to unwind after an active day on the force. That was ten years ago. Now as Pilaf's police chief, he continues with lessons from an artist in nearby Apple Creek. It's the creative outlet he uses to relax at the end of every day.

Mrs. Krumm returned to the lectern and announced that there was one more special guest speaker before Chef John emerged. She called on Dr.

O'Connor, who rose from his table and came to the lectern.

"Surely you've noticed that every place setting has a plate cover. There's something special underneath each one."

With that, Chef John's team filed out of the kitchen. As if they had carefully choreographed what happened next, each chef stood to the left of one of the ladies at every table. They ceremoniously reached for the top of the dish cover, and simultaneously lifted them off. On each dinner plate, there was simply a photograph of last week's meal with "2 Timothy 3:16-17" printed at the top. After all the plate covers were removed, the ten chefs paraded back into the kitchen and closed the door.

Dr. O'Connor continued, "Now don't worry. This is not your meal for tonight. As appetizing as the photo may be, eating a photograph would not exactly be tasty or satisfying."

Laughter rippled through the hall.

Dr. O'Connor continued, "However, it does have something to do with the Scripture verses you saw in the most recent artwork by Officer Caputo and on the top of the photograph.

"You see, we fuel our bodies several times every day. Praise God that it is a delightful experience. The sense of taste is a beautiful gift from God. But as God's creative handiwork, are we not more than flesh and bones? The immortal element of each of us is our spirit, that which animates the physical. If we are so diligent to feed our bodies, should we not feed our spirit daily with God's Word?"

Guest's heads were nodding with renewed understanding and smiling at the elaborate way in which this drama drew the town together.

Dr. O'Connor continued, "I invite everyone to church tomorrow. I'm starting a new series on how to develop and foster your spiritual hunger. Invite everyone you know. I guarantee that your spirit will be satisfied. But right now? I'm all for ministering to our bodies. Please bow your heads as we ask the Lord for His blessing on tonight's meal."

Dr. O'Connor invited the very presence of God at every table, and to bless the hands that prepared the feast. When he was done, every single enthusiastic voice offered a synchronous, "Amen!"

Mrs. Krumm returned to the mic and wasted little time. She simply introduced Chef John, who emerged from the kitchen to thunderous applause. When the long-lasting applause finally faded, he told everyone to save the photos as a reminder to feed both body and soul. Chef John's team then brought out his favorite dish, Beef Wellington, for everyone to enjoy.

The festive meal was overflowing with the kind of joy that made everyone want to linger well past dessert. There were still a dozen people chatting in fellowship hall when our family left at a few minutes past 11 o'clock.

Today feels like the day after Thanksgiving. Last night's meal was so complete and satisfying that a cup of coffee is all I need right now.

Pilaf's many questions were largely answered last night, but for me, one or two remain. How did Officer Caputo get the CLIP numbers for the initial stages of the artwork? And how many people beyond Officer Caputo and John Rowe did it take to pull off this complex, successful drama? I hope to find out when we all gather together for the last worship service of the year.

Sunday, December 31, 2017, 5:09 PM

The last bit of sun is about to disappear. Pilaf sunset is at 5:10 p.m., some 10 minutes later than the earliest sunset of exactly 5:00 p.m. for the first thirteen days of December. Unless one is paying very close attention, there isn't much discernible difference yet. All December nights are long and dark. We curse the darkness with Christmas lights of all kinds. Using light to celebrate Christmas is more than appropriate. A Great Light arrived on the scene over two-thousand years ago to provide a rescue line for anyone who believed it and grabbed on. 1 John 1:5 says that, "God is light, and in Him there is no darkness at all."

Imagine that! No shadows. None! Every nook and cranny of heaven is filled with God's glorious light. No more sunsets. No more long, dark, cold nights. The beauty of Christmas lights pale in comparison to the light that fills heaven.

That was part of the message Dr. O'Connor delivered to a completely packed church this morning, surrounded by a sanctuary full of beautiful Christmas lights. He suggested that we keep a mental picture of heaven's beauty ever-present in our minds, just like the photo of last week's beautiful meal at last night's dinner. It will keep our healthy hunger alive, a hunger that will keep us in God's Word.

Before the worship service, the Sunday morning Bible class played host to many new people. They were there because they were either a part of Chef John's dinner series, or they were captivated by the sequence of artwork showing up all across Pilaf. All of the regular attendees had read and meditated on Psalm 1 all week, ready for today's discussion. It has been a long time since that happened. To Chef John's credit, his elaborate strategy paid off in a way I never thought possible.

There was a lot of lingering after the service was over. Like last night's event, hardly anyone was anxious to leave. Instead, people were eager to digest the events of the last few weeks by talking with family, friends, and neighbors.

I eventually found Officer Caputo to ask him a question or two. During our conversation, I learned that a chain of information had to be established to get Joel and Jessie's CLIP number. It was Mrs. Krumm's idea. She remembered where they kept track of the daily number after asking them about it two years ago. She offered to visit the seventh grade homeroom to glean the number off Jessie's book cover. Then she called Mrs. Sauerkraut and gave her the number that Officer Caputo retrieved when he did his rounds. Mrs. Sauerkraut had no idea why the number was significant, but she knew it was part of an elaborate antic that had Pilaf talking. Since Officer Caputo was involved, the daily adrenalin rush of slipping a number to Pilaf's man in blue was better than a cup of coffee for the nonagenarian. In short, she got a charge out of it.

Officer Caputo told me that he almost clued me in on what was going on. When Uncle Ben, George, and I followed him into Mrs. Krumm's closed classroom to "investigate," he thought about briefing us on the elaborate plan. I remembered him raising his hand as if he was going to say something, but he waved off his own thought. Officer Caputo told me that had we been alone, he would have told me. He did not want the inner circle to be that large. As it was, his cover was nearly blown by two feathery troublemakers when Bonnie and Clyde managed to swipe some of his art implements as well as his belt badge.

Here it is, finally the last day of the year. Do I dare hope that the last six hours of 2017 will be uneventful? I think we've had enough drama in one month to fill an entire decade! Having a very, very quiet New Year's Eve is exactly what Pilaf needs. We are all so tired. I seriously doubt any one of us will make it much past 10 o'clock. It's just as well. I'm planning to watch the sunrise tomorrow morning with a cup of coffee in my hand, a warm, furry cat on my lap, and God's Word beside to me. I am still amazed that the Lord patiently waits for me every morning.

Monday, January 1, 2018, 7:22 AM

Happy New Year! There was no battle when we whisked everyone off to bed well before midnight last night. Jessie actually fell asleep on the couch just after 9 o'clock when we were all talking about the month's crazy events. I carefully scooped her up and carried her to her bedroom. While Jennifer changed her into her pajamas, I accompanied Joel into his room where I tucked him in like a snug cocoon. He fell asleep while I was praying. It wasn't long after that we were all dreaming of sugar plums. I could not have designed a better end to a calendar year.

I did wake briefly at 1:11 a.m. Mom and Dad must be smiling. I sure miss them. I'm glad it's only for a season.

Sammy is pawing at my lap. My coffee is hot. My Bible is open. Dawn is showing its best colors. The sun will soon wake Pilaf creating those long, lonely blue shadows along the snowpack. Someday, no more darkness, no more shadows. Until then, I'm thankful for the creative ways we can marginalize the dark, especially at this time of year. The lights. The sounds. The smells. The people.

It's Christmas in Pilaf.

Disclaimers, thanks, and all that extra stuff:

Certain names and places that appear in this fictional storyline may actually exist out there, somewhere, but the situations in which I placed them are all fictional, a product only of my zany, uninhibited creativity. Rest easy. All persons living in Pilaf, Ohio (located in a secluded sector of my imagination) are fictional characters. Any resemblance to anyone real, living or dead, is completely and totally random, a completely serendipitous fluke defying mathematical probabilities.

Thanks to someone very real: My editor Dawn Manausa. I would have waved the white flag after counting one-hundred typos, misspellings, grammatical errors. How you maneuvered through 683 corrections and suggestions is beyond me, not to mention helping me see the forest through the trees when I needed a storyline reset here and there.

Special thanks to Rev. Lud Golz of <u>Getting God's Message</u>. During our annual board meeting in September, he unknowingly gave me the Scriptural material that was essential in bringing Pilaf's mysterious artwork to life during the storyline's home stretch. I'll forever smile every time I read Psalm 119.

"For God so loved the world that he gave his one and only Son, that whoever believes in him shall not perish but have eternal life." John 3:16 (NIV)

Made in the USA
San Bernardino, CA
04 December 2017